"You're attracted to me."

Was he that easy to read? Jack kept his face expressionless. "Amazing."

"What?"

"That ego of yours. How'd you ever get something that big through the doorway?"

"It's not ego." Kelsey's green eyes met his. "I felt it—the pull between us. Are you going to tell me you didn't?"

Jack swallowed. Yes, he felt it. He didn't deny he was attracted to her. But just because he felt it didn't mean he had to act on it. He controlled his body and his heart, not the other way around.

Damn, but Kelsey was sexy. And tempting. And a distraction his instincts told him he couldn't afford.

Dear Reader,

I'm a small-town girl at heart, which is probably why so many of my stories are set in small towns. I live in the same rural hometown where I was born and raised, and I'm now raising a family of my own there. Like my hero, Jack, there's nothing better to me than having my family close by, knowing my neighbors and being an active part of my community.

To my heroine, Kelsey, there's nothing worse.

Being in Serenity Springs serves only as a painful reminder of Kelsey's troubled past. Until she learns to forgive herself for her mistakes and realizes that with Jack she has what she's always wanted—a family to call her own. And in Serenity Springs she has what she didn't even realize she needed—a place to belong.

The release of this book is the realization of a longtime dream to see one of my stories in print. I hope you enjoy reading about Jack and Kelsey as much as I enjoyed writing their journey.

I love to hear from readers. Please visit my Web site, www.bethandrews.net, or write to me at P.O. Box 714, Bradford, PA 16701.

Happy reading!

Beth Andrews

NOT WITHOUT
HER FAMILY
Beth Andrews

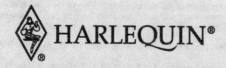

HARLEQUIN®

TORONTO • NEW YORK • LONDON
AMSTERDAM • PARIS • SYDNEY • HAMBURG
STOCKHOLM • ATHENS • TOKYO • MILAN • MADRID
PRAGUE • WARSAW • BUDAPEST • AUCKLAND

ISBN-13: 978-0-373-71496-4
ISBN-10:   0-373-71496-3

NOT WITHOUT HER FAMILY

This edition published by arrangement with Harlequin Books S.A.

® and TM are trademarks of the publisher. Trademarks indicated with ® are registered in the United States Patent and Trademark Office, the Canadian Trade Marks Office and in other countries.

www.eHarlequin.com

Printed in U.S.A.

ABOUT THE AUTHOR

Award-winning author Beth Andrews is living her dream, writing romance novels for Harlequin Books while looking after her real-life hero and their three children. A self-professed small-town girl, Beth still lives in the Pennsylvania town where she grew up. She has been honored by her kids as The Only Mom in Town Who Makes Her Children Do Chores and The Meanest Mom in the World—as if there's something wrong with counting down the remaining days of summer vacation until school starts again. For more information about Beth or her upcoming books, please visit her Web site at www.bethandrews.net.

For my Critique Partners, who so generously gave
their time, encouragement and unending faith.

For my kids, who proudly told people
I was a writer way before I ever did.

For Andy, who shows me every day
that real-life happy endings are possible.

ACKNOWLEDGMENTS

I'd like to thank Officer Harsen for his valuable
input. Any mistakes I've made are my own.

I'd also like to thank Victoria Curran for helping
to make this book the best it could be.

CHAPTER ONE

"MA'AM, I NEED YOU TO MOVE away from the counter and keep your hands where I can see them."

Damn. That didn't sound good.

Standing in a dim patch of light a foot away from the horseshoe-shaped bar, Kelsey Reagan slowly turned toward the deep, commanding voice.

As she did, her gaze slid over the tall man walking into the empty room. A blue T-shirt clung to his broad shoulders and he wore snug, dark blue jeans. Military-short black hair, granite features and icy-blue eyes completed the picture. All in all, a completely hum-worthy package.

She rolled her eyes. God, she really needed to get a grip. One look at a pretty face and she totally lost focus. She wasn't here to enjoy the scenery—as nice as it was. She was here to see Dillon.

Besides, gorgeous or not, this guy was so not her type. Even though he wore normal clothes instead of some god-awful uniform, Kelsey instinctively knew what he was. The authority in his voice, the way he seemed to size her up within seconds of looking at her, and his rigid, ready-for-anything posture told her he was a cop through and through.

Mostly it was the confident, *I'm legally entitled to carry a gun and, yes, I will shoot you if you piss me off,* tilt of his chin that gave him away.

"I'm with the Serenity Springs Police Department," the cop said in a grave tone as he fished something out of his back pocket.

Kelsey sighed. She'd done it again. Wrong place. Wrong time. Her official, unofficial motto.

She should have it tattooed on her ass.

Except this was the right place. The Summit Bar of Serenity Springs, New York. As for the time…well…considering how long she'd waited to see Dillon again, and how desperate she was to make amends with him, it was the right time. It had to be.

She waved her hand at the shiny silver shield the cop held up for her inspection. "You can put the tin star away. I already pegged you as a cop."

He pocketed his badge, his gaze intense as he studied her. "Ma'am," he said evenly, "this establishment is closed."

She rolled her eyes again at him calling her *ma'am*. At twenty-seven, she was a good eight years away from official membership in the Ma'am Club.

"Okay, I realize this…" She trailed off as she took in the scarred tables and chairs, walls discolored from years of cigarette smoke and the ancient linoleum floor. Establishment? Who was he kidding? This place was a dump, pure and simple. "I know this…bar is closed, but I figured there must be someone here."

"What, exactly, led you to that conclusion?"

"Because when I knocked, the door practically swung open."

He raised one dark eyebrow. She pursed her lips. Shoot.

Looked like she was digging herself deeper and deeper into a hole.

She should've waited outside for Dillon instead of letting herself into the bar, especially once she realized the place was empty. But she'd been so excited to finally see him again— and afraid he'd take off if he spotted her in the parking lot.

Probably not the smartest move. Then again, she wasn't exactly noted for her decision-making skills.

She ran the tip of her tongue over her dry lips and saw the cop follow the movement. Noticed a small, but real, flare of awareness.

She narrowed her eyes. Seemed to be a spark of life beneath this guy's steely exterior after all. Maybe she could still wriggle her way out of this mess.

She hated to brag, but she was a damn good wriggler.

And while she'd done her best to avoid any contact with the police in the past ten years, wriggling with this particular cop wouldn't be too much of a hardship.

She attempted a smile. "Look, Officer—"

"Actually it's chief. Chief Jack Martin."

Her grin slid away. Of course he was the chief. Because no way could she be lucky enough to get busted by a lowly traffic cop or something.

She tried again. "*Chief* Martin, my name is Kelsey Reagan and I don't know what you think—"

"What I think," he interrupted smoothly, "is that you're trespassing on this property. You could be looking at breaking-and-entering charges."

Her stomach fell to rest somewhere in the vicinity of her big toe.

"Hey, whoa, back up the paddy wagon there, Sheriff. This

is all a big misunderstanding." She worked to keep her voice light and steady and prayed she projected the right combination of honesty and innocence. Sort of like a Girl Scout. They were all about honesty and innocence, right? Which probably explained why she'd never been one. "I didn't break in here. Not really."

"How do you *not really* break in to a place?"

"Like I said, the door wasn't locked and—"

"Do you always walk into a building simply because the door's not locked?"

She fought her growing irritation. "What I'm saying is that I'd hoped someone was here so I knocked, several times, and when no one answered—"

"You let yourself in," he finished for her. "Despite the Closed sign on the door."

"I didn't come inside to steal anything. I'm actually looking for someone who works here."

"That so? And who would that be?"

"Dillon Ward." She bit the inside of her lip. "Maybe you know him?"

He didn't so much as blink. Kelsey blew out an exasperated breath. Didn't everyone know everyone in a small town? But there was no flash of recognition in the cop's eyes.

"Look," she said, setting her purse on the bar, "I have a picture of him in here, maybe you could—"

"Hold up." Chief Martin closed the distance between them in two long strides, picked up her purse and dumped it on the bar out of her reach.

Her mouth fell open. "What was that for?"

"A precautionary measure."

"For what?" Then realization dawned on her and she

wasn't sure if she was amused or offended. "You worried I have a gun in there? Sorry to disappoint, but I left my Uzi in my evening bag."

Ignoring her, he finally stepped back and nodded toward her scattered belongings. "Go ahead."

She started to speak, then decided against it and dutifully pulled her wallet out of the mess and flipped it open. She took out the ten-year-old picture of Dillon and handed it to the cop but couldn't stop herself from asking, "You always such a tight ass? Or is this just my lucky day?"

"Just doing my job, ma'am." He glanced at the picture. "What's your business with Mr. Ward?"

Kelsey cleared her throat. "It's personal."

He handed the picture back to her. "We've had several burglaries and instances of break-ins resulting in destruction of property over the past two months and—"

"I hate to burst your bubble," she said as she tossed her stuff back into her purse, "but I've only been in town an hour. Any destruction to this property was done long before I arrived—maybe even before I was born. Besides, what am I supposed to steal? Plastic sip straws?"

She snapped her purse shut, raised her head and bit back a yelp of surprise. Chief Martin had stepped closer, his large body now looming over her. In an instinctive attempt to put some distance between them, Kelsey shuffled back and found herself pressed against the bar.

Her heart galloping in her chest, she straightened and forced herself to maintain eye contact. Cops were like wild dogs—hostile, arrogant, downright mean—and they ran in packs. The police department in her hometown had rallied around her abusive stepfather for years, simply because he was one of them.

She also knew if you showed them the slightest hint of fear, they'd gobble you up before you could say "kibble."

"I wasn't accusing you of any wrongdoing, ma'am," he said in that annoyingly calm, emotionless voice of his. "I was simply explaining the reasons behind my actions."

"Oh." Kelsey swallowed and berated herself for attempting to antagonize him. "Sorry. It's just that you…I mean… cops…make me nervous," she blurted, her face heating.

His expression didn't change. Did the man ever blink? "I take it you've had your share of run-ins with the police?"

"You could take it that way."

Way more than she was comfortable with—starting with her first arrest at age ten for shoplifting. During the next five years she'd been busted for almost everything including underage drinking and vandalism to resisting arrest. And each time, when her stepfather—Glenn—found out about the trouble she'd gotten into, she usually ended up with a few bruises as part of her punishment.

"Seeing as how the owner isn't here, and taking into account the break-ins, why don't I just wait with you until Mr. Ward arrives?"

Kelsey crossed her arms. Just once she'd like real life to go according to her plans. Nowhere in her itinerary for the day did she have *hang with a cop* penciled in.

It grated to admit that even after all these years, cops still made her nervous. And she still didn't trust a one of them.

She shook her head. "That's not really necessary—"

"I insist," he said, his steady blue eyes meeting hers.

She tried to tell herself her unsettled stomach was caused by nerves but even she wasn't that good a liar. Okay, she really did not need her previously dormant hormones to surge to life. Not now. And especially not with a cop.

"You know," she said, ignoring the unsteadiness in her voice, "maybe I should just wait in my car. Then we can chalk this whole episode up to one big misunderstanding."

She wasn't sure, but she could've sworn his lips twitched. "But this episode was just getting interesting," he said dryly.

Yeah. That's what she was afraid of.

"Besides," he continued, "you never explained what your personal business with Mr. Ward happens to be. Is he your husband? Boyfriend?"

She shook her head. "No. He's my brother."

HER BROTHER? He hadn't seen that one coming.

She didn't look much like the broad-shouldered, dark-haired Ward. Jack took in Kelsey Reagan's slim legs, subtly curved hips and the tight black T-shirt hugging her small, round breasts. And was that a tattoo peeking over the waistband of her low-slung jeans?

His mouth grew dry at the idea of finding out, and he frowned. *Focus, Martin.*

He stole a quick look at her left ring finger. "Is Reagan your married name?"

"I'm not married."

"Divorced?"

She raised both eyebrows. "Nosey, aren't you?"

Warmth crept up his neck but he merely shrugged. "Just curious."

"If you must know, Dillon is my half brother. Different fathers."

"And, as Mr. Ward's sister, you thought illegal entry was a good idea?"

She sighed. "You're just not going to let that go, are you?"

"I'm just doing—"

"I know, I know. You're doing your job. I get it, okay? Just lay off the *ma'ams*," she said as Jack's sister Allie walked through the front door, "or else I might give you a reason to haul out those handcuffs you're obviously dying to use."

"Hey," Allie called, curiosity clear on her face, "what's going on?"

Ignoring his sister—and Kelsey's loaded statement about him wanting to cuff her—Jack kept his gaze on the redhead. She reminded him of those modern art paintings his daughter had been fascinated with at the Metropolitan Museum of Art a few months back. The sharp lines of Kelsey's face shouldn't have worked with her high cheekbones and narrow nose. But they did. In fact, her unique features made her face all the more interesting.

He frowned. He found her interesting in a totally professional way, he assured himself, nothing more.

"I need to speak to the building's owner for a minute," he said, stepping back. But it wasn't far enough away to avoid her light, citrusy scent. "Why don't you have a seat?"

Her emerald-green eyes narrowed. "I'll stand."

Intrigued by her stubbornness, he kept his mouth shut and walked over to where Allie stood, halfway into the bar.

"What's going on? I thought you had the day off," Allie said softly. She set two plastic grocery bags on a table, looking from him to the redhead and back again. "Who's that?"

"I am off duty." Jack turned so both the redhead and the

exits were within his sight. "I came over to see if you wanted to have lunch."

"You mean you came over to see if I'd cook you lunch."

He almost grinned. "Only if you insist."

Allie cuffed him on the shoulder. "That still doesn't answer my second question. Who is she?"

"Says her name is Kelsey Reagan. Ring any bells?"

Allie glanced at Kelsey again. "No. Should it?"

"I just figured since you and Ward are such good buddies, you'd know the name of his sister."

Allie's eyes widened. "You're telling me this Kelsey…"

"Reagan," he supplied.

"Kelsey Reagan is Dillon's sister?" At Jack's nod, she continued, "He's never mentioned her. Not to me, anyway."

Jack didn't miss the surprise on Allie's face. Ever since Ward, the ex-con-turned-carpenter, started renovating The Summit, rumors had spread around town that he and Allie were lovers. But if that was true, surely she'd recognize the name of Kelsey Reagan.

Not that Jack believed the gossip. And not just because he didn't want Allie involved with someone with Ward's less-than-desirable background. No, he based his conclusions on the only thing he could count on. Cold hard facts.

While Allie had never bothered to deny or confirm it, the few times Jack had been around the two of them, he'd seen nothing to indicate their relationship was anything other than friendship. There were no long looks. No subtle brushing of hands. No sparks.

Nothing even remotely close to the flash that had, briefly, arced between Jack and Kelsey a few minutes ago.

He rubbed a hand over his face. "Upon entering the

premises, I discovered Miss Reagan inside. She claims the door was unlocked—"

"It was unlocked," Kelsey called. "And if you're going to keep talking about me, you might want to either lower your voices or go into another room."

Jack took hold of Allie's arm and moved her farther away from the bar. "Is that true?" he asked quietly.

Allie shrugged out of her red leather jacket. "I didn't lock the door when I left, if that's what you're asking."

"How do you expect to run a business when you can't even remember to lock the door?"

"I didn't *forget* to lock it," Allie whispered, "I left it open because I didn't know when Dillon would be back."

He glanced back at Kelsey. "I think it would be a good idea for you to check around, make sure nothing's missing."

Allie frowned. "Why? I only ran out for a few minutes."

"In those few minutes, you could've returned to find half your stock gone and your cash register empty."

"The stock's still here," she said, motioning to the bottle-filled shelves behind the bar. "Was she emptying the cash register when you found her?"

A headache began to form behind his eyes. "No. But that doesn't mean she didn't help herself to your petty cash."

"It doesn't mean she did, either." She laid her coat on the table. "Remember that pesky little constitutional amendment? The one about a person being innocent until proven guilty?"

Spoken like the defense lawyer Allie was. Or had been until she'd chucked eight years of higher education, quit her job and returned home to buy this run-down bar.

Talk about your less-than-stellar career moves.

"Let's save the debate on criminal rights for another time. Just do me a favor and check the cash register. Please," he added, knowing Allie would balk at anything she construed as an order.

With a resigned—and to Jack's mind, overly dramatic— sigh, Allie crossed the room and went behind the bar. Sending Kelsey an apologetic look, she opened the cash register drawer, glanced down and shut it again. She shook her head at Jack.

"I told you I didn't steal anything," Kelsey said with a smirk. And if he thought the smirk was sexy, no one had to know but him.

"Ignore my brother," Allie told her. "He's a bit overprotective." She smiled. "I'm Allie Martin. Jack says you're looking for Dillon?"

"That's right. I thought he'd be working here today."

"He ran out for some lunch," Allie said. "But he should be back any minute. Can I get you something? A soda, maybe?"

"Uh…" Kelsey's eyes darted from Allie to Jack, but then she slid onto a stool. "A soda would be great. Thanks."

Allie filled a glass and placed it in front of Kelsey. "Is Dillon expecting you?"

Kelsey twirled her straw between two fingers. "I doubt it. I was in the area and thought I'd drop in to see him." She sipped her drink. "So…uh…you own this place?"

"I do." His sister's pride was unmistakable. And, if you asked Jack, unwarranted.

Not that he wasn't thrilled to have Allie back in Serenity Springs where she belonged, but why couldn't she have opened a law practice instead of mixing drinks for a living? Or at least bought a place that hadn't sat empty for the past year?

Allie leaned her elbows on the bar, her chin in her hand. "Actually I've only had it a few months. Dillon just started the renovations and he figures it'll be at least two months before we're done."

"Have you thought of moving the pool table there?" Kelsey pointed to the far corner by the kitchen. "It would open the flow of traffic and leave you room for more seating."

"You think?"

Kelsey nodded. "Yeah. That way you could put in a small dance floor as well. You could even add a dartboard."

Jack sat two stools down from Kelsey and zoned out of their conversation before they started swapping decorating tips and cake recipes. His instincts went into overdrive when he looked at Kelsey. It was more than just her looks, her clothes and her bad-girl vibe.

He'd been brought up to never judge a book by its cover. Helen and Larry Martin had raised their four children to be fair and nonjudgmental. His liberal mother insisted on tolerance and compassion, and his father—Serenity Springs' previous chief of police—truly believed justice was for all.

Nice sentiments, but Jack knew better.

Nine years working the streets of New York City, working his way up to detective, had wiped away any idealistic beliefs his parents had instilled in him. Tolerance and compassion were no match against the endless stream of violence and ugliness so many people faced day in and day out.

He'd learned to look beyond the obvious. To count on his instincts. At the moment, those instincts were telling him there was more to Kelsey Reagan than met the eye.

"What the hell are you doing here?"

Jack turned to see Dillon Ward standing in the doorway.

Ward's usual cold, flat expression had been replaced with a dark scowl. And that dark scowl was aimed at none other than Kelsey Reagan.

Jack glanced at Kelsey. Gone was the cocky, go-to-hell attitude. Instead she seemed apprehensive. Nervous. Almost... vulnerable.

What was that about?

Kelsey got to her feet. "I...I wanted to see you."

Her statement was met with silence. Not the comfortable kind, either. More like the oppressive, somebody-say-something-to-break-it kind.

"Well," Allie said brightly, doing her part to ease the tension in the room. "I'm starving. I think I'll just go make some lunch. Come on, Jack."

"I'm not hungry." He kept his eyes on Ward.

Allie walked around the bar and stopped in front of Jack. "I said—" she grabbed his arm and pinched, hard "—let's go."

Ow. Damn, that was going to leave a bruise. "Fine." He twisted out of her reach knowing he could keep an eye on Kelsey and Ward from the kitchen. Allie grabbed her coat while Jack picked up her groceries.

"What was that for?" Jack asked when they were in the kitchen.

"What do you think?" She unloaded her groceries onto an old, large farm table. "They don't need us watching their every move."

"Wanna bet?"

She sent him an exasperated look. "You're overreacting, Jack. Just because you don't like Dillon—"

"He's a convicted felon. A murderer."

Allie's expression darkened and she slammed a can of tomatoes onto the table with more force than necessary. "Dillon has paid his debt to society, and he's been an exemplary citizen since he moved here. Besides, whatever's going on between him and Kelsey is none of our business."

"As chief of police, everything that happens in this town is my business." He edged toward the doorway to watch the couple in question. "But, as long as Ward and his sister keep their noses clean, they won't have anything to worry about, will they?"

KELSEY MET DILLON'S HAZEL EYES and emotions surged through her, too numerous to name, too frightening to acknowledge. The only solid thought she could grasp and recognize was that after so long, she was finally face-to-face with her brother again.

Too bad she'd only been fooling herself all these years thinking time would heal their wounds.

Maybe she shouldn't have come. She barely recognized Dillon as the young man who'd given up his future for her. In his place stood a broad-shouldered stranger who looked at her with cold, emotionless eyes.

Well, one thing was for sure. He hadn't been expecting her.

Guess she should've remembered how much he hated surprises.

"What do you want, Kelsey?"

"Leigh's dead," she blurted out as she twisted her fingers together. "She died in her sleep three months ago. The coroner said it was heart failure."

"I know."

She dropped her hands to her sides. "You do?"

"Yeah."

And here she'd thought the news of their mother's death would be the perfect excuse for tracking him down.

"If that's what you came here to tell me—"

"I just wanted to see you. To talk to you." No response. Not a flicker of emotion crossed the hard planes of his face. "Uh, how have you been?"

"You mean since the last time you saw me?" He stuck his hands in his front pockets and shrugged. "Hard to get much worse than being in federal prison, isn't it?"

She flinched at the bitterness in his voice. At the accusation. Of course he had every right to accuse her. After all, he wouldn't have gone to prison if he hadn't been protecting her.

She wanted to beg him to forgive her for what happened. To throw herself into his arms and never let him go again. Instead, she took several deep breaths and wiped her damp palms down the front of her jeans.

"I can't believe it's been ten years," she said. "It's taken me so long to find you." Silence. She forced her lips into a smile. "You're a hard man to track down."

"That's the way I wanted it."

She dropped her pseudo-grin. Okay. Things weren't going quite as well as she'd hoped. Not only had she forgotten how much Dillon disliked surprises, but she'd also forgotten how bullheaded he could be.

She glanced toward the kitchen, not surprised to see the cop watching them from the doorway. "Is there somewhere we could go to talk?" she asked Dillon.

"I'm working," he said flatly.

"Dillon, please—"

"No. I'm not interested in anything you have to say. You shouldn't have come."

She willed back tears. She kept her voice low and fought the urge to turn and run away from the hatred in his eyes. "I just want a chance to talk to you, to apologize—"

"I don't care what you want. Not anymore." He met her eyes. "I want to be left alone. To forget everything that happened."

Though it hurt—God did it hurt—Kelsey forced herself to ask, "Does that include me, too?"

"Yeah," he said after a long moment. "It does."

It was like being punched in the gut. She was shocked to find she was still standing, still on her feet and able to breathe when all she wanted to do was slide to the floor and cry. "Please, I—"

"No." He pinched the bridge of his nose before letting his hand drop. "Look, I don't blame you or hold you responsible for what happened, but the past is over. And I want it to stay that way."

"It doesn't have to be over. We can work through this. Start again."

He shook his head and turned to leave.

She reached out, her fingers grazing his hand. "Dillon, wait. We could—"

He whirled around and grabbed her by the upper arms. She gasped as he raised her onto her toes. "Damn it, Kelsey." He shook her once. Though it was the barest of movements, it made her stomach turn. "Don't you get it? I'm through with you."

"Is there a problem, Ward?"

Kelsey shut her eyes at the sound of the cop's commanding voice. When she opened them again, the cop was standing behind Dillon, his expression downright frigid.

Dillon dropped her arms and stepped back. "No problem, Chief Martin. Kelsey was just leaving."

She pressed her lips together. "You want me gone? Fine. But we aren't done yet."

Kelsey spun on her heel and stormed out into the bright sunshine. Crossing the paved parking lot, she passed a run-down pickup truck, a snazzy red SUV and the cop's car—a black-and-white Jeep. When she reached her ancient gray hatchback, she bowed her head and inhaled shakily. She rubbed her hands over her arms where Dillon's fingers had been, unsure if she was shivering because of the cool October breeze or Dillon's anger.

"You okay?"

She stiffened. "Fine." She swiveled to face the cop. "Don't tell me I'm breaking some sort of city ordinance by standing in one spot too long."

He studied her silently and she could've sworn he looked… concerned. For her.

"I wanted to see if you were okay," he said. "All part of the job."

The job. Of course. What, had she honestly thought he'd been worried for her? Ha. Fat chance.

"Well, thanks. I guess."

When he didn't say anything else, she turned back to her car, pulled her key out of her front pocket and inserted it into the lock with an unsteady hand. The urge to escape, to run away, almost overwhelmed her. Had her pulse racing, her palms sweating. She didn't want to stay, didn't want to face her mistakes or her brother's disgust.

But she couldn't run. Not this time. She wouldn't give up. No matter what Dillon said or how many times he pushed her away, she wasn't going anywhere until she got what she came for.

It wouldn't be easy, she'd known that much before she'd left New York. What she hadn't taken into account was how much it would hurt to look into Dillon's eyes and realize the truth—he hadn't forgiven her. For putting him in the position where he'd had to take a man's life to save hers. And for abandoning him.

How could she ever forgive herself?

CHAPTER TWO

JACK COULDN'T HELP BUT WONDER what was going on in Kelsey's head. He'd only been in her company less than twenty minutes but he already knew she was a puzzle.

He always did like solving puzzles.

Hell, the biggest mystery at the moment though was why he had followed her out here in the first place. Sure, he'd told her he was just doing his job, and after seeing Ward manhandle her, that was partly true. But he was also there because, to be honest, he didn't like the vulnerability he'd seen in her any more than he'd liked the sight of that SOB grabbing her.

She slid him a sideway glance. "Quit looking at me like that."

She sure was prickly. Come to think of it, prickliness and defensiveness were two of Ward's more irritating traits as well. Guess there was a family resemblance after all.

"How am I looking at you?" He hoped it wasn't with anything other than professional interest. He hadn't given himself away, had he?

She faced him, her pretty green eyes flashing. "With pity."

"I don't pity you." Though he hadn't liked how she'd clearly lost her confidence and spirit when Ward had stepped into the room. "I don't think Ward's worth it."

"Not worth what?"

Not worth the tears he'd seen in her eyes or the dejection in her expression.

"Not worth getting so upset over," he said. "I've seen Ward's kind before. You're better off without him."

Her mouth opened. Then shut. She shook her head. "You don't know Dillon or me. And I don't need, or want, your opinion."

He probably deserved her curt tone. Even it he'd only been trying to help. But if she wanted to waste her time with the likes of Dillon Ward, it was no concern of his.

"I apologize if I was out of line," he said, unable to keep the stiffness out of his voice. With a slight nod, he put on his sunglasses, turned and walked away.

He wasn't going to apologize for distrusting Dillon Ward. Of course, it was true that Ward had managed to stay out of trouble since being released from federal prison, but Jack wasn't about to let his guard down. Especially while Ward was working for Allie.

"Hey, wait a minute," Kelsey called, exasperation clear in her voice.

Jack stopped by his Jeep and slowly turned around. She was still at her car, her arms crossed at her chest, her mouth turned down at the corners.

"Was there something you needed?" he asked when she remained silent.

Her frown deepened and she sighed heavily which, for some crazy reason, made him want to smile. He must really be losing it.

The sun picked up the copper highlights in her spiky hair

as she trudged across the parking lot toward him. "I need directions to a place to spend the night."

"Planning on staying in our fair town long?"

"Don't worry, Sheriff. I'll be gone in the morning."

He wasn't worried. Much. "Depending on what you're looking for—"

"Just a clean bed and bit of privacy."

"You might like the B and B over by the lake. The Bee Hive."

She snorted. "You're kidding, right?"

"Afraid not." He opened the Jeep's door, pulled out his citation book and ripped out a ticket. After scribbling directions on the back, he handed her the paper. "It's clean and not too far from here."

She hesitated a moment before taking it, careful not to touch him.

"Thanks," she said, avoiding his eyes. Jack leaned back against his car as he watched her march away. She climbed behind the wheel of an older model gray compact and took off like a redheaded bat out of hell.

He blew out a breath, climbed into his Jeep and told himself he was glad Kelsey was leaving in the morning. Though there might have been a small spark of attraction between them, it was only temporary and superficial. Not that he minded superficial when it came to sex, but even if Kelsey did stay in town, he'd keep his distance from her.

The last thing he needed, he thought as he started the ignition, was to get tangled up with Dillon Ward's sister.

KELSEY STAGGERED INTO HER ROOM, turned the lock on the door handle, crossed the small space and fell facedown onto the plush bed. The room was sparsely furnished but clean.

There didn't seem to be many other options in town. At least not many she could afford. Which Chief Martin had obviously figured out or else he wouldn't have suggested this place.

She sighed. It was one thing to be down and out. It was another to be obvious about it. Not that she cared what he thought of her. He was just another guy in uniform.

She turned her head to the left and wrinkled her nose. Oh, all right—the cop was gorgeous. In a law-abiding sort of way. And yeah, there had been a moment when she'd felt a definite…connection. Not one of those eyes-locked-across-a-crowded-room moments or anything. More like an awareness. And she was pretty certain he'd felt it, too.

And that he hadn't liked it any more than she did.

She yawned widely and shut her eyes. It was barely 5:00 p.m. and she was already bone weary, which was so unlike her. For the past three years she'd tended bar during peak hours so she was used to being up late. But the emotional roller coaster she'd been riding since discovering her brother was alive and well—and living a few short hours away from her—left her exhausted.

Too bad their reunion hadn't gone as smoothly as she would've liked.

She rolled onto her side and stared at the sky-blue wall. The color reminded her of the cop's eyes so she turned onto her back, absently picking at the bedspread.

She'd shocked Dillon by showing up unannounced, but she'd been scared he'd take off if he knew she'd found him. She couldn't take the chance of losing him again. Once Dillon calmed down, he'd listen to her. Her hand fisted in the bedspread. He had to.

She'd been a senior in high school the last time she saw him. She'd ditched class and taken a bus to the Toledo Correctional Institute where Dillon was serving his sentence for manslaughter. He'd been so distant, so cold. As if she'd meant little more to him than a stranger would.

She had no one to blame for the distance between them but herself. Because he'd had to save her, Dillon spent close to five years locked up.

Dillon told her he didn't want her to visit or write him again. She'd let him push her away, had allowed her pain—and her guilt—to keep her away.

Even then, she never gave up on him. She'd found an attorney willing to take his case, one who'd been able to get his sentence reduced. But by the time she'd gotten up the courage to face him again, Dillon had disappeared from Ohio and her life.

She hadn't come this far—literally and figuratively—to give in now. She wanted her brother back in her life. Wanted to prove she wasn't the same impulsive troublemaker she'd been. Mostly, she wanted a connection to the only person who'd ever believed in her. Who'd ever loved her. And, by God, that's exactly what she would get.

Whether Dillon liked it or not.

"BUY ME A DRINK, SAILOR?"

Jack glanced up. "Not in this lifetime."

"Pinching pennies?" Seth Valentine sat on the bar stool next to Jack. "No wonder you never get laid."

"(a) You're not my type," Jack said over the classic Aerosmith song playing on The Summit's jukebox. "And (b) I've had sex plenty of times without your half-assed advice."

"I'm not talking about your solo sessions. Only the times another warm body was involved. And barn animals don't count."

"You're a riot," Jack told his closest friend. The bartender, a heavily made-up brunette with a silver hoop in her left eyebrow, took Seth's beer order and scurried off. "What are you doing here? The NYPD now giving detectives weekends off?"

Seth scooped a handful of bar nuts from the bowl in front of them. Tossed some into his mouth and shook the ones left in his hand. "Came up for my mom's birthday tomorrow."

"She still pissed about Mother's Day?"

"She threatened to sell her house and move in with me if I miss her birthday, and I have to get her a decent gift."

Having known Mrs. Valentine since he was in kindergarten, Jack knew she didn't issue empty threats. "Guess that six-month membership to Weight Watchers wasn't such a hot idea."

"Hey, she's always moaning about losing twenty pounds. How was I to know it would set her off?" Seth nodded his thanks when his draft was placed in front of him. "What about you?" he asked, wiping his hand on his jeans before picking up his beer. "Where's Emma?"

"She's spending the weekend with her grandparents."

Ever since his wife died in a car accident four years ago, Emma spent one weekend a month with Nicole's parents in New Jersey—Jack wanted his daughter to stay connected to both sides of her family.

Seth, in the act of raising his beer, stopped suddenly and whistled under his breath. "Hello. Look what just walked in."

Jack followed his friend's line of sight. His stomach did one slow roll.

Conversation quieted as every eye in the bar zeroed in on

Kelsey. With her tight jeans and spiky red hair, she begged attention. She'd changed into a long-sleeved, purple T-shirt and, as she strode into the room, her small breasts bounced beneath the fabric.

He couldn't help but enjoy the sight.

"I'd kill to see those legs in a skirt," Seth said in an undertone. "A really short skirt with a pair of three-inch heels. And those have got to be the perkiest pair of—"

"Shut up," Jack murmured as Kelsey drew near. Her eyes locked on his for a moment as she passed him by. He turned and watched her perch on a stool at the far end of the bar before tearing his gaze away.

"What?" he asked, noticing Seth smirking at him.

"Anything you want to tell me?"

"No."

"Then I'll just ask. Who is she?"

Jack finished his soda and set the glass on the bar. "Why so interested? She's not exactly your type."

"I happen to love redheads."

"Since when?"

"Since I found true love with sweet Mary Jane Hanover."

Jack snorted out a laugh. "Is this the same Mary Jane whose very large boyfriend kicked your ass for sleeping with her?"

Seth swallowed a drink of beer. "He wasn't her boyfriend at the time. I don't poach."

"Unless you won't get caught."

"Unless I won't get caught," he agreed. "And I didn't get my ass kicked. I held back so I wouldn't hurt that idiot."

"Whatever helps you sleep at night. Anyway, as I remember, sweet Mary Jane wouldn't give you the time of day, let alone any sexual favors, until I buttered her up for you."

"Please—" Seth held a hand out to stop him. "Don't use expressions like *buttered up* when talking about Mary Jane. Gives me ideas. And don't think you can get away with changing the subject, either."

Jack hooked his foot on the rung of his stool and debated the chances of getting Seth to drop this discussion. He bit back a sigh. Not going to happen. Seth's laid-back attitude and humor hid a tenacity unrivaled by mere mortals. "Her name is Kelsey Reagan and she's Dillon Ward's sister."

"Ward... You mean the guy who lives above the bakery?"

"One and the same." He glanced over to see Kelsey talking to the bartender. "She's only in town for the night."

Seth grinned. "Too bad. You could—"

"Hello, gentlemen," a female voice purred.

Jack turned and found himself looking into a pair of dark-blue eyes. "How are you, Shannon?" he asked the beautiful blonde.

"Couldn't be better," she replied in her husky smoker's voice. "I was wondering if I could buy you a drink?"

"Would you look at the time?" Seth didn't bother glancing at his watch as he drained his beer. He stood and tossed a five dollar bill on the bar. "I'd better get going." He flashed a grin at Jack. "Catch you later."

Jack clenched his teeth as his ex-friend cheerfully abandoned him. Wasting no time, Shannon claimed the empty stool. Her short, black skirt rode a few inches above her knee to show a good deal of her toned, tanned thigh. She shook her long, golden hair behind her shoulder and looked at him from under her lashes.

As far as sultry looks go, hers was top-notch. Jack wondered if she practiced it in the mirror.

"What'll it be?" she asked.

He'd have one quick and painless escape, please. Unfortunately, his position as police chief, and hers as the wife of a prominent city councilman, made running like hell an impossibility.

Too bad.

"Thanks, but I'm not drinking tonight," he said.

She looked pointedly at his empty glass.

"That's fine," she assured him, leaning forward. Though he suspected she was giving him a clear view down the V-neck of her silky white shirt, he kept his gaze on her face. "I wanted to talk to you about the security for the country club's Harvest Ball."

Sure she did. And thirteen-year-old boys snuck peeks at *Playboy* for the articles.

The headache he thought he'd got rid of earlier began to come back. He blamed it on Shannon's perfume, something floral and overly sweet. Remembering Kelsey's fresh, sexy scent, he glanced in her direction. Humor lit her expression as their eyes met.

Jack broke eye contact first and turned his attention back to Shannon. "Everything's all set for the dance. If you have any questions, we can go over them at next week's meeting."

"Those meetings are always so hectic." She pouted and laid a well-manicured hand high up on his thigh, her red fingernails stark against his jeans. "Why don't we go back to my house? We can discuss it now."

Her lips said *discuss*, but her eyes said let's get naked and do the nasty.

Jack groaned inwardly. Polite tact was lost on Shannon. He lifted her hand off and stood.

"I'm sorry but I already have plans." He kept his voice low, controlled and, though it almost killed him, pleasant. "Now, if you'll excuse me, I see someone I need to speak with."

Ignoring the angry flush staining Shannon's cheeks, he turned and walked to the end of the bar. He wasn't sure which was worse, the way Shannon blatantly came on to him whenever they were in the same room together. Or the fact that to escape Shannon, he was heading straight for Kelsey Reagan.

He stopped next to Kelsey's stool and waited until she looked up. "Mind if I join you?"

Kelsey glanced behind him then back. "Using me as an escape hatch, Sheriff?"

"I'm not the sheriff." Jack sat next to her. "I'm the chief of police."

She waved that distinction away. "Whatever you are, you've surprised me."

"How so?"

"By not being interested in Tropical Tan Barbie over there. Most men would sell their soul to have a woman like that coming on to them. Either you're one of the few faithful married men alive—"

"I'm not." As usual, when he thought of Nicole he felt a slight pinch to his heart. When Kelsey raised her eyebrows he added, "I'm not married."

She tilted her head, watched him thoughtfully. "Oh, well then. Maybe you're just not into women."

What the hell? He straightened and tried to laugh, but the idea of a sexy woman thinking he was gay was about as non-funny as you could get. "I'm not gay."

The humor lighting her eyes told him she knew damn well he was straight. She'd just been yanking his chain. "What's the matter then? Jeez, she was practically drooling in your lap."

"For some reason, drooling desperation doesn't turn me on."

"Huh. Go figure." The bartender came over and slid a plate of cheese-covered French fries in front of Kelsey.

"What brings you back to The Summit?" he asked when they were alone again.

"I was hungry," she said and popped a dripping fry into her mouth.

"And, besides clogging your arteries, you wanted another shot with your brother."

She swallowed then took a sip of her drink. "Wow. That's brilliant detective work. You should be a cop or something."

Jack's lips twitched.

"You, on the other hand," she continued, wagging a fry at him, "are not only hiding from the blonde, but you're also checking up on me." She leaned toward him, her citrus scent tickling his nose. "Shouldn't you mutter something about this town not being big enough for both of us?"

He lifted a shoulder. Eased back to put some distance between them. "Too cliché for me."

The amused look on her face told him she noticed how he'd backed away from her. "Don't worry. I won't tell anyone your secret."

"I already told you," he said quietly, "I'm not gay."

"No kidding. But that's not what I'm talking about. And the real reason you're over here isn't because you're running from the blonde."

"It isn't?"

"Nope."

Jack waited. She dug in to her food with the enthusiasm

of a linebacker three times her size. Though his gut told him he would regret asking, he couldn't stop himself. "Are you going to enlighten me?"

"You're attracted to me."

Holy hell. Was he that easy to read?

He kept his face expressionless, his voice dry. "Amazing."

"What?"

"That ego of yours. How'd you ever get something that big through the doorway?"

"It's not ego. I felt it—the pull between us. Are you going to try and tell me you didn't?"

He swallowed. Hell yes, he felt it. The attraction between them wasn't exactly subtle. Physical and momentary, yes, but not subtle.

But just because he felt it, didn't mean he had to acknowledge it. Or worse, act on it. He controlled his body, and his feelings, they didn't control him.

He deliberately straightened and shifted so that their knees brushed. Her startled gaze shot to his. At the quick, telltale nervous gesture of her pink tongue wetting her lips, his stomach tightened.

Damn, but she was sexy. And tempting. And a distraction he couldn't afford.

"Let's cut to the chase," he said.

"Okay. You first."

The pulse at the base of her neck beat rapidly. He had the strongest urge to press his lips against it.

He jerked his head up. "I'm not over here because I'm attracted to you."

"No?"

"No. After your foray into breaking-and-entering this afternoon, I'm over here to make sure you keep your nose clean while you're in my town."

"Don't worry, Sheriff, like I said I won't be in your town much longer. Besides," she added with a quick, lethal smile that made his heart skip a beat, "other than that little misunderstanding, I usually avoid trouble at all costs."

He studied her, looking for subterfuge beneath the humor. She sure as hell seemed sincere. So much in fact that for some crazy reason, Jack found himself wanting to believe her.

He straightened where he sat. Damn it, he couldn't ignore his instincts, not again. And if he let his guard down for one moment, he'd give in to his attraction to her. And that he couldn't afford to do.

CHAPTER THREE

THE DISBELIEF ON JACK'S FACE told Kelsey he didn't trust her. She shrugged and dug back into her food to hide her embarrassment. So much for her vow to think before she spoke.

She was supposed to be proving she could curb her impulsive and reckless tendencies. Guess she still needed practice.

"So, you walk the straight and narrow?" Jack asked.

Finished with her fries, Kelsey wiped her mouth with a paper napkin and tossed it onto her empty plate. "Haven't had so much as a parking ticket in the past ten years."

"That's quite an accomplishment."

"It's more of an accomplishment for some than others."

"Looks like you're going to get your wish," Jack said.

"What wish is that?"

He gestured to the door. Dillon stood across the room, his eyes on her. Luckily, the same blonde who'd tried to pick up Jack stopped Dillon before he could leave. But, if Kelsey didn't hurry, she would lose her chance to talk to her brother tonight.

She jumped off the stool, dug some money out of her front pocket and tossed it on the bar.

"Do you think that's a good idea?" Jack asked.

"I just want to talk to him."

"You tried that once."

"Yeah, well, I don't give up easily." But the idea of Dillon blowing her off again kept her rooted to her spot.

Biting her lower lip, she looked back at her brother. His expression darkened as he listened to the blonde now hanging on his arm. Dillon's mouth thinned but he didn't shake her off. Instead, he met Kelsey's eyes for one long moment, turned on his heel and led the blonde out the door.

Dillon was gone.

"I'd heard there was bad blood between them—your brother and Shannon," Jack said, bringing her attention back to him. "Something about a job he did at her house. Guess whatever the problem was, it's fixed now."

"Gossiping, Sheriff?"

Her toes curled at the grin he shot her. "Everybody here knows everybody else's business." He leaned toward her and lowered his voice. "Especially their secrets."

She swallowed. Jack's face was inches from her own, his blue eyes so mesmerizing, she was unable to look away. Suddenly everything was too much. The noise in the bar. The number of people. And especially Jack, sitting close enough for her to feel his body heat, his expression knowing and intense.

"It's getting late," she pointed out. "I'd better head back to the B and B."

Jack got to his feet. Kelsey stepped back and bumped into the stool in her haste to make sure their bodies didn't touch. Other than a slight quirk of his lips, he gave no indication he noticed.

"I'll walk you out," he said.

She shrugged and turned away but knew he was right behind her. When he laid a hand on the small of her back to guide her through the bar, she almost jumped out of her skin. The warmth of his fingers seeped through her shirt and a shiver rushed up her spine.

They stepped outside into the cool evening air and Jack dropped his hand. She immediately missed the contact.

"Where are you parked?" he asked.

"Over by that second light." Kelsey dug her keys out of her purse. "Aren't you worried about your reputation?"

"Not particularly. Why?"

"Well, everyone in the bar saw us leave together. What if they think we're heading back to your place for a marathon round of wild jungle sex?"

She felt, more than saw, him glance at her. "They'll think what they want," he said after a long moment, "whether it's true or not."

"I'd rather not know a single soul than have everyone talking about me, knowing about my personal life."

"Once you get used to it, a small town's not so bad."

"I know exactly what it's like. The town I grew up in isn't much bigger than Serenity Springs."

"You don't miss it?"

Miss everyone looking down their noses at her, knowing her every mistake? Hardly. "No. I'd rather be in New York. Look at all it has to offer. Starbucks. Krispy Kreme. Excitement. Variety."

"There's nothing about the city you don't like?"

She could do without her supervisor, Eric, giving her the worst shifts at the club and cornering her every chance he got so he could rub his insignificant self against her. But she couldn't blame that on the city. Just her own stupidity for breaking her *"No sleeping with the boss"* rule and getting involved with Eric in the first place.

She stopped beside her car, unlocked the door and faced Jack. "New York is the biggest, most exciting city in the world." Which was absolutely true. Even if she did, at times, feel lost and alone. "What more could I want?"

JACK COULD THINK of something *he* wanted. And he wouldn't have to go far to get it, either. A quarter of an inch, half an inch max, and he'd be able to capture her mouth with his.

He didn't move.

If he moved, he'd have to touch her. And touching her was the last thing he needed to do.

He fisted his hands. Kelsey remained motionless, her full lips tipped up in a half grin, her body trapped between him and the car.

He tamped down a surge of desire. "Serenity Springs is nice. Small. Quiet."

"You mean boring."

"The security of knowing your neighbors more than makes up for any perceived boredom. The predictability is comforting."

"It's comforting to you."

He stuffed his hands in his front pockets. "I lived in New York. Nine years of crowds, pollution and, of course, the never-ending crime." He shook his head. "I'll take small town any day."

She leaned back against her car. "You're forgetting all the good things about it. Dance clubs, museums, live theater. The bustle of the crowds."

He snorted. "Homeless people. Worrying some lunatic is going to push you out in front of an oncoming train."

"This town doesn't even have a Chinese restaurant, which means no kung pao chicken or pot stickers. That's just wrong. Not to mention un-American."

He coughed to cover his laugh. Jack loved living here, but he knew not everyone did. A lot of people were biding their time until they could move on to better things.

Except he'd experienced the supposedly bigger and better and had found it to be neither. Besides, this was the best place to raise his daughter. She needed the security. They both did. And coming back here was what had gotten him through that first year without Nicole.

"It's like you already said," Kelsey continued, "you can't do or say anything without the entire town knowing about it. Plus, they know exactly who and what you are. Even if you wanted to change, they won't let you. What if you wanted to do something out of character? Cut loose?"

What he wanted was to nibble on her lower lip, to run his tongue over it before sucking it gently into his mouth.

And she knew it. He could see it in her eyes. The awareness.

He had to put her in her car and get the hell out of there. Before he did something totally stupid. "I don't want to cut loose." Maybe if he kept saying it, he'd start to believe it. "It's getting late, you'd better go."

Disappointment flickered in her eyes, but she straightened. "Right. Well, thanks for walking me to my car."

He didn't know why, but he couldn't let her go. Not yet.

"Wait," he said and she looked at him expectantly. "I'm not sure I trust you," he told her.

Instead of being offended, she nodded. "Ditto."

So why were they leaning in toward each other? Why couldn't he stop himself from reaching for her, from placing his hands on her lower back and pulling her to him?

Her eyes widened, her pupils grew big, and though he gave her plenty of time to draw away from him, she didn't. Their bodies met. Her hip pressed against his thigh. Heat spiraled through his body. Jack couldn't seem to keep his hands still. He stroked her long back, moving under the edge of her shirt to caress the skin at the gentle curve of her waist.

Her skin was warm. And soft. He slowly dragged his hands up her arms and over her shoulders. She tipped her head back as he trailed his fingertips over the rise of her collarbone. Cupping her throat, he ran the rough pad of his thumb over her lower lip.

She trembled. He watched, transfixed by the movement of his thumb over that plump lip. The very tip of her tongue flicked against his skin. Dark, powerful lust punched him in the gut.

Fighting for control, he slid his hand around the back of her neck and tightened his free arm around her waist, pressing her intimately against him.

"You're still leaving tomorrow, right?" he asked, his voice rough.

She stroked her cool fingers across the back of his neck. "First thing in the morning."

Good. If she wasn't going to stick around, he could appease his curiosity. He could satisfy his craving for her.

Then he'd be able to banish her from his thoughts.

"I can't think of anything I'd rather do at this moment than kiss you," he admitted.

"You don't trust me," she reminded him, her hands moving up his chest and linking behind his neck.

True, but that didn't seem to matter. Not when his hands were on her and she was looking up at him, her eyes a dark, mossy green, her body pressed against his.

Promising himself just one quick taste of her, he fisted his hand in her short hair. Some part of his brain recognized how the fragrant strands slipped through his fingers like silk, but then he lowered his mouth to hers and stopped thinking altogether.

HEART POUNDING IN ANTICIPATION, Kelsey kept her eyes open and on Jack's as he closed the distance separating them. He brushed his lips against her mouth. Once. Twice. Three times. Her eye fluttered shut when he settled his mouth on hers.

She sighed softly. Yes. This is what she'd wanted.

Contrary to the hunger that practically emanated from of him, he didn't devour her, didn't overwhelm her. Despite his hand on her head and his arm around her waist, he kept the kiss gentle. Soft. Controlled.

He raised his head, breaking contact. "That was a mistake."

Kelsey lifted her heavy lids and blinked away the thick haze of desire. That was it?

Jack stared down at her, his expression hot with want, his mouth tight with tension. He began to pull back, removing his hand from under her shirt.

Oh, no. No way. She tightened her grip on him. He wasn't going to back away now. She wouldn't allow him to pretend that meager excuse for a kiss had been enough for him.

Damn it, she wanted satisfaction.

"Yeah, that probably was a mistake," she agreed. And she pulled his mouth back to hers.

His deep groan reverberated against her lips. He slanted his warm mouth over hers as he took command of the kiss, deepening it until her limbs grew heavy and her head light. She was drowning in sensations, the rasp of his tongue against hers, the scrape of his whiskers on her face, the strength of his hands as they cupped her rear and held her tight to him.

She ran her hands over his shoulders and down his arms. Her need to get closer was so intense, she wanted to climb on top of him. Wanted to wrap herself around him, to absorb him through her skin.

The sound of music and voices floated over to them and Jack sprung away from her. Kelsey collapsed back against her car as a middle-aged couple left the bar. She watched them get into their car and pull out of the parking lot.

She glanced up to find Jack staring at her. She couldn't have moved even if she'd wanted to. And she didn't want to. She wanted to reach for him, or better yet, for him to reach for her. The last thing she wanted was for this moment to end.

Still trying to catch her breath, she ran her tongue over her lips. He squeezed his eyes shut. She didn't miss the way his chest rose and fell rapidly or how his hands were clenched into fists.

She waited until his eyes were open before speaking. "Too bad I'm leaving tomorrow. Imagine how much fun we could have if I stayed."

"That's what I'm worried about," he muttered and took another step back. "Goodbye, Kelsey."

Frustrated, and—if she was being honest with herself—relieved, she straightened. She'd managed to crack Jack's rigid control—and had the added bonus of the best kiss of her life—but he obviously didn't want to pursue this.

Which was for the best, really. Even if she couldn't help but wonder how good they'd be together.

Well, at least she hadn't begged him to take her home. Which meant she still had her pride. And while pride wouldn't keep her warm tonight, wouldn't keep the loneliness at bay, it would help make her exit a bit more dignified.

"Goodbye, Jack."

She got into her car, turned on the ignition and did the smartest thing she'd ever done in her life.

She drove away.

HE RUBBED THE BACK OF HIS NECK and glanced at his watch. 4:00 a.m. Jack's grim reflection stared back at him from the large picture window in Mark and Shannon Crandall's living room. He knew death was inevitable, just as he knew murder was inescapable. But the past few years in Serenity Springs had somehow lulled him into a false sense of security. Tonight he'd been shoved back into reality.

The house was quiet, the air thick and permeated with the coppery scent of blood.

He turned slowly and took in the stark room. White walls. White carpet. White furniture. A small black end table and a matching coffee table in the center of the room. Black-and-white photos of city skylines were framed in black and lined up with military precision on the wall behind the love seat.

The only splashes of color came from a few shiny red pillows on the sofa, a dozen long-stemmed roses on the end table and the bright red apples in a black bowl on the coffee table.

And the pool of blood staining the plush carpet beneath Shannon Crandall's head.

Jack crouched down. The position of the body—facedown between the sofa and coffee table, left leg slightly bent, arms splayed to the side—indicated she'd been hit from behind. Had she known she was in danger? Been trying to run away from her assailant?

It was obvious she was naked beneath the short, silky black robe she had on. Her pale hair was wild and tangled, matted with blood and brain matter. Jack shifted and forced himself not to cringe at the extent of damage done to Shannon's once lovely face. He scanned the area around the body, noting several streaks of mud and a partial muddy footprint on the floor.

He straightened. "What happened?"

Officer Ben Michaels wiped a trembling hand over his mouth. "I received an emergency call approximately thirty minutes ago. I arrived at the residence and found…" His gaze dropped to the dead body on the floor, his face losing color.

"Deep breath, Michaels," Jack commanded and physically turned the kid away from the body. Why did it seem like the least competent person in the department was always the first to arrive on the scene? "Who called it in?"

"The victim's husband." Michaels's light-brown hair stood on end as if he'd repeatedly run his fingers through it. Sweat dotted his forehead and upper lip. But at least he no longer seemed in danger of puking or passing out. "He's in the other room."

Jack glanced at the doorway that led to the brightly lit kitchen. "Did you discover any signs of forced entry?"

"No, sir. Mr. Crandall let me in. He said he spoke to his wife on the phone around one-thirty to let her know he was coming home early from a business trip. He said the door was locked when he arrived. He used his key to gain entry, found the victim and called 911. The EMTs arrived a few minutes after I did."

"Did anyone touch the body?" he asked, hoping no one had compromised the crime scene. "Did anyone move the body? Touch anything in the room?"

Michaels shook his head and shoved his hands into the bulky pockets of his police-issue Windbreaker. His gaze once again strayed to Shannon. "No, sir. Once the EMTs arrived and it was obvious Shan…I mean the victim was…gone…the EMTs escorted Mr. Crandall into the kitchen while I waited for backup."

Jack nodded. Considering this was undoubtedly Michaels's first murder scene, he'd done surprisingly well. Poor kid was taking it hard, though. Hell, the entire town was going to take the murder of one of their own hard. Serenity Springs was known for skiing, tourism and small-town charm. There was hardly a bevy of criminal activity.

Which was why Jack had returned here to raise his daughter in the first place.

Thank God Emma was with her grandparents. Knowing she was being taken care of, knowing she was safe, made it a hell of a lot easier for him to focus on his job.

Especially when his job was to track down a murderer.

"Good work," Jack told Michaels. "Now I need you to go outside and help canvass the yard. Don't overlook anything, no matter how insignificant it might seem."

"Yes, sir," Michaels said, clearly relieved.

"Medical examiner's on his way, Chief," Officer Nick

Pascale said as he joined Jack. Unlike Michaels, the burly, gray-haired Pascale barely looked at Shannon's body. He handed Jack the department's camera kit. "State police have been notified as well."

"Good. Who's in the kitchen with Crandall?"

"Flick and the EMTs."

Jack turned on the digital camera and recorded the date, time and his location on the front page of his notebook. "Make sure they all stay in the kitchen. I don't want any foot traffic in this room unless it's absolutely necessary. And if Crandall so much as has to take a piss, he's escorted, got it?"

"Will do." Pascale nodded toward Shannon. "Terrible thing to happen to such a pretty girl."

Jack's stomach twisted as he looked down at her lifeless body through the camera's viewfinder. "Terrible thing to happen to anyone."

Pascale lowered his voice. "The husband seems pretty shook up. You think it's an act?"

"That's what we need to find out, isn't it?"

Pascale made a grunt of affirmation. Clicking the shutter, Jack flashed back to when Shannon had come on to him at The Summit. It wasn't exactly a secret that Shannon fooled around on her husband, or that Mark preferred to turn a blind eye to his wife's infidelities.

Had that changed tonight? Had Shannon's unfaithfulness pushed her husband to do the unthinkable?

And what about the man Shannon had left the bar with? Had the ex-convict lost control of the violence Jack sensed lurked just beneath the surface? Dillon Ward had killed before. It wasn't much of a stretch to think he was capable of taking a woman's life.

As he methodically snapped pictures, Jack couldn't help but remember the kiss he and Kelsey had shared.

He lowered the camera fractionally and clenched his jaw. Damn it, he never should have touched her.

Didn't matter, he assured himself as he raised the camera. By the time he was through processing the scene and went to question Ward, Kelsey would be long gone.

CHAPTER FOUR

KELSEY SMOOTHED A HAND over her jittery stomach before inhaling deeply and knocking on the door to Dillon's apartment. She'd almost left town, had made it as far as the highway before deciding to try one more time to get through to her brother. She needed to tell him how sorry she was for her part in sending him to prison.

And she needed him to listen. But, even if he did blow her off again, she wasn't giving up. She'd simply go back to Manhattan and regroup.

Lifting her hand to knock again, she heard footsteps and the door opened. Her heart sank. Dillon looked like hell. Heavy stubble coated his cheeks and chin, his eyes were bloodshot and he had a serious case of bed head.

He looked like their stepfather used to after one of his many benders.

She swallowed her disappointment. God, how she wished his life had turned out differently.

It would have turned out differently, she reminded herself, if it hadn't been for her.

"I thought you were gone." Dillon's voice was husky, as if she'd woken him up. Possible, since it was barely seven-thirty on a Saturday.

"I'm leaving," she said, pushing past him, but her entrance was ruined when she stumbled over a pair of work boots by the door. She kicked them to the side and stepped over several small clumps of mud littering the floor.

"Come on in," he said wryly as he shut the door.

Kelsey crossed to the small, round kitchen table. "I just need ten minutes."

"I told you yesterday—"

"Please, Dillon. I swear, after ten minutes, after you hear me out, if you still want me to leave, I'll go. You'll never have to see me again."

She held her breath while he studied her. Time had matured him. Besides his broader shoulders, his face was much leaner. But his eyes, those incredible hazel eyes of his, were the same.

This *was* the same brother who had loved her.

"Ten minutes." He went to the sink and began filling a coffeepot with water. "Then you're gone."

She pressed her lips together and sat at one of the two chairs at his table. While he measured out coffee, she looked around the apartment. It was small and sparsely furnished. No clutter on the counters, no pictures or photographs on the walls. No magnets or notes littering the refrigerator. Pretty much just like her own apartment.

And how sad was that?

"This is a nice place," she lied.

Dillon snorted. "It's a regular penthouse."

"Have you lived here long?"

"Long enough."

She forced a smile even though Dillon had yet to look up from the coffee dripping into the pot. "Smells good up here.

Must be nice living over a bakery. Bet you get all the day-old stuff half price, huh?"

He finally lifted his head. "You're rambling."

Heat crept up her neck. "Yeah, well, I ramble when I'm nervous."

He grunted and replaced the pot with a mug so the brewing coffee dripped directly into it. Poured coffee into a second mug before putting the pot back and set one in front of her. "I remember."

And for some stupid, inconceivable reason, those two little words made her eyes fill with tears. Luckily, Dillon turned back to the coffeepot and she was able to blink away the offensive moisture before he noticed.

He pulled the other chair out and sat down. "Why don't you—"

A knock at the door cut him off. Dillon swore under his breach and went to answer it, his body blocking Kelsey's view.

"Holy God," he said to the person on the other side. "Could this morning get any worse?"

"I need you to come to the station with me."

Kelsey froze. She recognized that voice. It had haunted her dreams last night. Well, maybe not her dreams, more like her fantasies.

Dillon opened the door more fully. "I'd love to, Chief. But I'm afraid I have company."

Jack entered the room, his gaze zeroing in on her. "What are you doing here?"

"She's leaving," Dillon said, before she could speak, "in approximately four minutes."

Jack frowned and turned his attention back to Dillon. "She's leaving now. And you're coming with me."

Dillon sipped his coffee, leaned back against the counter and crossed his bare feet at the ankles. "What's this about?"

Jack quickly studied the room, then stared at a spot by the door. "Are those your boots?"

"Yeah."

"Were you wearing them last night?"

Dillon straightened. "Why?"

Jack looked at Kelsey as he said, "We can discuss it at the station."

She fought a growing sense of unease. "I think you should discuss it now."

"This doesn't concern you, ma'am," Jack said.

Ma'am? Last night the man had kissed her as if he couldn't get enough of her and now he was back to calling her *ma'am?*

She looked out the open door. A uniformed officer stood on the top of the stairs. Her unease turned into full-blown panic. "If it involves my brother, then it does concern me."

"Take it easy," Dillon murmured to her. "Am I under arrest, Chief?"

"I just want to ask you a few questions about last night."

"Ask away," Dillon said mildly.

"Where were you this morning between the hours of midnight and two-thirty?"

"I was here."

"Can anybody verify that?"

"Not that I know of."

"I, along with numerous other witnesses, including your sister here—" Jack nodded toward Kelsey "—saw you leave The Summit bar with Shannon Crandall."

"So?"

"Were you in Mrs. Crandall's house?"

"I stopped by there—to pick up a check."

"Did you and Mrs. Crandall argue?"

Kelsey couldn't keep quiet any longer. "What's this about?"

Jack kept his eyes on Dillon. "Shannon Crandall was found murdered this morning."

Her stomach turned. "What? Oh my God. But, I don't understand." She looked from Jack to Dillon as they attempted to stare each other down. Jack's face was unreadable, while Dillon's expression grew darker with each passing moment. "What does this have to do with Dillon?"

"Don't you get it?" Dillon ground out harshly when Jack remained silent. "I'm their number-one suspect."

JACK SHUT THE DOOR TO the booking-interrogation room after taking Ward's statement, leaving Pascale in the room with their suspect. Alone in the hallway, he leaned against the cold beige wall and stared at the scuffed linoleum floor.

Two hours of questioning and they hadn't managed to shake Ward's story or, better yet, get him to confess.

Ward had been nothing if not cool and calm during the past two hours. No matter how hard Jack had grilled him, he'd stuck to his story unflinchingly, his expression giving none of his thoughts away.

And, as much as Jack would like to blame the lack of progress on Ward's stoic personality, he couldn't help but wonder if it was his own fault. If coming back to Serenity Springs had somehow dulled his edge as an interrogator. An edge he'd honed carefully during his four years as detective.

With little physical evidence—and no murder weapon— no eyewitnesses to the actual crime, and no confession, he didn't have a strong enough reason to charge Ward with murder.

Yet.

Jack walked past the empty holding cells and down the main hallway. As he placed his hand on the doorknob to the break room, Ben Michaels came barreling around the corner.

"Chief," the kid called as he hurried down the hall.

Jack sighed. "What's the problem?"

"Dora Wilkins is here…out front. She wants a statement."

Jack rubbed his temples. Because not only was Dora editor in chief of the local newspaper, the *Serenity Springs Gazette,* she was also their lead reporter. And a huge pain in Jack's ass.

He ground his back teeth together. Hell, he'd hoped for a few minutes alone. Time to make a quick phone call to his in-laws and check in on Emma. "Put Dora in my office. Tell her I'll—"

"I can't do that," Michaels blurted.

"Why not?"

Michaels's protruding Adam's apple bounced as he swallowed. "I've already put my mom…uh…I mean, the mayor in your office."

Great. Not only did he have a murderer to find and an over-zealous reporter to get rid of, but he also had to take time to coddle and reassure Mayor Michaels.

Sometimes, he really hated his job.

"Does Dora know the mayor is here?" Jack asked.

"Not that I know of."

"Keep it that way. Let the mayor know I'll be in to see her in five minutes. Then put Dora in the front office. Tell her I'll give her an official statement in half an hour. Any word from the district attorney?"

"He's in court this morning, but he's supposed to call as soon as he has a recess."

Jack turned to the break room door. "Let me know the minute he calls."

"Uh, Chief…"

Jack bit back a curse. "Yeah?"

"That woman, the one who was at the accused's apartment—"

"He's not the accused. He hasn't been charged."

"Right. Uh, anyway, she showed up here after we brought Mr. Ward in." He lowered his voice and gestured to the door. "She's waiting in there."

Of course she was.

So far he'd managed to put Kelsey—and the stricken expression on her face when he'd escorted her brother to a police car—out of his mind. Naturally he would now have to face her, to be reminded of the way he'd lost control and kissed her.

Kissing her had been a mistake. He just hadn't expected it to reach this magnitude of mistake-dom. After all, last night she'd simply been a sexy stranger. A woman who'd attracted him.

Today, she was the sister of a murder suspect.

"Better make it fifteen minutes before I get to the mayor," Jack said. "And no one on staff talks to Dora. No statements. No theories. Nothing. If she so much as asks for the time, the answer is 'no comment.' Understand me?"

Michaels bobbed his head. "Yes, sir."

Jack pushed the door open.

Kelsey, in the act of pacing behind the long, scarred rectangular table, whirled to face him. "It's about time. Can my brother leave now?"

Ignoring her question—and the way her scent wrapped around him—he headed to the coffeemaker. After pouring the inky liquid into a disposable cup and adding a generous amount of powdered creamer, he grabbed the bottle of pain relievers from the counter.

After downing three pills, he looked at her. Held up his cup. "Want some?"

"I don't want any coffee," she snapped. "I want answers."

He sat at the table. "Have a seat."

"I'll stand."

He wasn't about to discuss anything while she hovered over him like a damn storm cloud. Jack sipped his coffee and watched her steadily over the rim of his cup.

It didn't take long for her to get the message. She huffed out a breath before sliding a chair out with her foot and perching on the edge of her seat.

"Where's Dillon?" she asked.

"He's signing his statement."

She visibly paled. "A statement? He's giving a statement without a lawyer present?"

"You've been watching too many television cop shows. He doesn't need a lawyer—"

"Anytime someone gets dragged down to the police station, they need a lawyer."

"He wasn't dragged anywhere. He came willingly. And he doesn't need a lawyer because he's not under arrest."

She stood. "Great. That means he's free to leave."

He was, but if there was a legal way to hold Ward, one that wouldn't jeopardize any future charges against him, Jack would do it in a heartbeat.

"We're not charging him," he admitted. "You might want

to convince him it would be in his best interest not to take any sudden trips out of town."

Her eyes narrowed to green slits. "What's that supposed to mean?"

"Your brother is a person of interest in an ongoing murder investigation. It wouldn't look good if he were to suddenly disappear."

"This is ridiculous." She slapped her hands down on the table and leaned toward him. "You're harassing him for no reason."

He met her eyes, eyebrow raised. "Murder is a pretty good reason, don't you think?"

A flush reddened her cheeks. "Look, just because Dillon was seen leaving the bar at the same time as that woman—"

"That woman had a name," he said quietly. "And now she's dead."

Kelsey swallowed and something shifted in her eyes, but she didn't back down. "You're looking to pin this murder on someone and Dillon is a convenient target."

He finished his coffee and prayed for the painkillers to kick in soon. "Are you insinuating the only reason we brought your brother in for questioning is because he's killed before?"

She flinched and straightened quickly, a guilty expression on her face. Did being reminded of her brother's past upset her so much? Or, could it be that despite her protests, she was worried Ward could be guilty of this murder, too?

"Is this how you run an investigation?" she asked. "Placing blame on someone because of their past?"

"If that person's past is significant—which in this case it most certainly is." He rested his arms on the table and clasped his hands together. "You have to face facts. Your brother was the last known person to see Shannon alive."

"He didn't kill her. I know he didn't."

"He's already admitted he followed Shannon home."

"That doesn't prove anything."

"He also admits he and Shannon argued."

That shut her up. But only for a minute. "Doesn't matter. You're looking at the wrong person."

"For your sake," he said sincerely, "I hope you're right."

He rose and tossed his empty cup in the trash. For some reason that he didn't want to examine too deeply, he hated the thought of her being involved in this mess.

"You know," he said, "the best thing you could do is forget all of this. Go home, go back to your life."

"I want to see my brother. Now."

Damn, but she was stubborn. And loyal. How would she take it once that loyalty to her brother was proved unfounded?

"I'm sure Ward is almost ready to leave," he said. "I can send someone in to get you—"

"Don't bother." She stalked past him and opened the door. "Just tell Dillon I'll be waiting for him in the parking lot."

Before she could leave, Jack caught her by the wrist. "I'm telling you, for your own good, you don't want to get tangled up in this, Kelsey. Go home."

Without waiting for her to respond, he dropped her wrist and walked out the door.

IN THE SMALL PARKING LOT behind the police station, Jack's parting words played through Kelsey's mind as she paced under the midday sun. No matter what he said, she wasn't going anywhere.

She needed to stay and help prove Dillon's innocence. To make sure he wasn't railroaded for a crime he didn't commit. No way would she sit back and do nothing while her brother went to prison.

Not again.

The door opened and Dillon walked outside followed by a flabby, middle-aged cop. God, how many times growing up had the situation been reversed? How many times had she been escorted out of the local police station only to find Dillon waiting for her?

Too many. Way too many. After all, she'd been the juvenile delinquent.

Dillon must've read her mind because when he noticed her he said, "Just like old times, huh?"

"Not funny." She fell into step beside him, aware of the cop following close behind them. "Come on. I'll drive you home."

Dillon shook his head. "I'm not going home."

"Where are you going?"

"To the hospital."

"What?" She stopped and grabbed his arm. "Are you hurt? Did they do something to you?"

"Relax," he said, peeling her fingers off him. "They didn't break out the rubber hoses. I'm going to submit a DNA sample."

"Voluntarily?"

His gaze flicked to the cop who now stood about thirty feet away next to a police cruiser. "Sort of."

While she wasn't sure it was in his best interest to submit a sample, she bit her tongue. "I'll go with you."

"No, thanks."

Okay. He obviously still didn't want her around. Too damn bad. "Look, I'm going to help you whether you like it or not."

He grimaced. "I don't like it."

"Tough. And what the hell are you thinking? Bad enough you're going to give them DNA, but I can't believe you gave them a statement without an attorney present."

"I don't need an attorney. I didn't do it."

"I know that," she said, but nothing changed in his eyes or on his face. No visible relief at knowing she believed in him. "What about the local public defender?"

He walked away, his long strides forcing her to hurry to keep up. "They offered to call him in, but I refused."

"Don't worry. If they insist on continuing with this bogus investigation, we'll hire the best defense attorney—"

"No."

"What? Why not?"

He stopped and frowned down at her. "I don't want or need your help. There's no reason for you to get involved. Or to stick around."

Kelsey slid a glance to the cop, not fooled by the way he stared straight ahead. She knew he was hanging on their every word.

She lowered her voice. "I'm not going to leave you."

"It's been a long time, Kelsey." Dillon sent her a cool look. "I'm not the same person I was back then and I'm not your problem to worry about."

"You're my brother," she said softly around the tears clogging her throat. "I love you."

She read something in his eyes. Something that looked like regret. Or perhaps, sadness. Whatever it was, it told her Dillon wasn't as unaffected by her words as he'd like her to believe.

"You shouldn't," he said simply, a breeze ruffling his hair. "You need to go back to your life and forget about me."

He climbed in the back of the police car. The cop shut the door, got in the front and drove away.

Kelsey slowly made her way across the parking lot to her car. She climbed in, started it and pulled out into the street. She made it three blocks before she had to pull over. Gripping the steering wheel with shaking hands, she battled back her tears.

She wiped her eyes. She'd help prove Dillon's innocence because, damn it, he was innocent.

Kelsey had to believe it. If she didn't, if her brother really was a heartless, cold-blooded killer, she had no one to blame but herself.

CHAPTER FIVE

IT WAS BAD ENOUGH HE couldn't get her out of his head, but a man was in deep trouble when he could still taste a woman after two days. Two days and two long, restless nights.

Sunday morning Jack jogged around the corner onto Main Street. Traffic was light, a few early risers making their way to church or out for breakfast. The crisp air along with the physical exertion helped to clear his head. The surrounding mountains with their patchwork of autumn colors and the steady sound of his feet hitting the concrete were reassuringly familiar.

God knew he could use some familiarity right now. He hadn't left the station until almost 1:00 a.m., only to spend another two hours at his kitchen table going over his notes and the pitiful amount of evidence gathered at Shannon's murder scene.

The only solid piece he had so far was that Mark Crandall's alibi panned out. Phone records proved that Crandall called home on his cell phone around one-thirty that morning, and eyewitnesses placed him at the airport at that time.

Since the airport is a good two hour drive from Serenity Springs, it was looking less and less like Mark Crandall had killed his wife. But that didn't mean he hadn't had someone kill her.

But he hadn't tossed and turned all night long just because of Shannon's murder.

An image of Kelsey entered his head and he increased his pace until his lungs felt like they were going to explode and his leg muscles screamed. From what Pascale told him of Kelsey's brief conversation with her brother in the parking lot yesterday, Ward had, once again, pushed his sister away. It must've worked this time as she never returned to the station. Word through the town's reliable grapevine was that she'd checked out of The Bee Hive, too.

Good, he thought as he passed A Word In Hand, the local bookstore. He didn't need that kind of distraction. He hadn't wanted it since Nicole died.

He experienced a twinge of regret but pushed it aside. His attraction to Kelsey was simply because of his recent dry spell.

He snorted as he crossed Kennedy Street. Dry spell? Seven months wasn't a dry spell. Seven months without the pleasure of a warm, sweet smelling woman was a damn drought.

Obviously his celibacy had affected his brain. Why else would he want a woman who was the exact opposite of what he needed? Not that he ever planned on needing another woman. Needing Nicole, loving her only to lose her had almost destroyed him and Emma. He couldn't take the chance of them getting hurt again.

Emma was happy and well-adjusted, even if she had been making noises lately about wanting a mother. He'd do anything to make his daughter happy.

Anything but that.

Because to get Emma a mother meant he'd have to get himself a wife. He could never replace Nicole, so why bother trying?

Kelsey intrigued him, that was all. But no more. He needed to stop thinking about her. Stop wanting her. He'd concentrate on solving Shannon's murder, and that would be a hell of a lot easier to do without his inappropriate attraction to the prime suspect's sister.

At the next corner, Jack scanned for traffic before crossing the street, and jerked to a stop so suddenly, if he were a cartoon character he would've left grooves in the sidewalk.

He blinked. Kelsey, wearing jeans and a white shirt with huge sparkly red lips on the front, was storming toward him. He slowed to a walk to catch his breath. Sweat rolled off his forehead and stung his eyes but he ignored it.

Pulling his T-shirt out from where he'd stuck it in his waistband, he wiped the sweat off his chest and face and tugged it on.

"What are you doing here?" he asked gruffly.

She waved a crumpled newspaper under his nose. "What the hell is this?"

He raised his eyebrows. Took the paper from her. "Looks like a copy of yesterday's *Serenity Springs Gazette.*"

She crossed her arms. "That's not yesterday's edition of the rag you call a newspaper. It's today's."

"The *Gazette* doesn't come out on Sundays."

"It did today. And I'll tell you something else, I'm going to make sure Dillon sues, not only the paper, but the Serenity Springs Police Department. Maybe even the town itself."

His stomach dropped. What the hell had Dora printed? He tried to smile, cool and detached. "I'm sure whatever's been reported is—"

"See for yourself."

It was thinner than usual, only four pages, but Kelsey was

right. It was a special Sunday edition of the *Gazette*. Jack glanced at the front page, and cursed softly. He quickly skimmed the article, his mood worsening with each word he read.

Dora had crossed the line this time. Bad enough she'd written a one-sided piece about Ward and his past murder conviction, she'd also printed information about the ongoing investigation that Jack hadn't wanted the public to know yet.

"Well?" Kelsey demanded.

He raised his head. "I didn't write this," he managed through clenched teeth.

"No, but you're directly responsible for it."

"How do you figure that?"

The breeze picked up, cooling his skin and mussing Kelsey's hair. "It's your case," she said. "Your information."

"I gave a statement, pure and simple. And this—" he waved the paper "—wasn't it."

His statement sure as hell hadn't included the fact that several items, including a beer bottle, had been sent to the state lab for DNA testing. Or that the mud found on the living-room carpet had been sent to the lab as well.

And he never mentioned that his department had yet to find the murder weapon.

"Then you have a leak in your department. They've essentially tried and convicted Dillon in that article. You might as well put out an open call for vigilantes to grab their ropes and hunt him down."

He folded the paper. Handed it back to her. "A bit dramatic, don't you think?"

"No." She snatched the paper out of his hands. "This is defamation of character."

"You think I'm happy about this? I'm trying to build a case here. Do you really think I wanted that information made public?"

"What I think, is that you'll do anything to pin this murder on my brother."

When she'd accused him of the exact same thing yesterday, he'd managed to let it roll off his back. Now, red-hot anger pumped through his veins. He had the mayor and entire city council riding his ass to make an official arrest. He also had the state police making noises about taking over the investigation, and now the details about the murder being splashed across the *Gazette*'s front page.

Damn it. He had enough going on at the moment, he didn't need crap from Kelsey, too.

He took a menacing step forward, only slightly mollified when her eyes widened and she backed up.

"If you have a problem with what's been reported, I suggest you write a letter to the editor," he said coolly. "But don't you ever again, even so much as hint that I would knowingly, willingly send an innocent person to jail or try to railroad someone for a crime they didn't commit."

KELSEY SWALLOWED. Oh, my. A pissed off Jack was…impressive. His eyes were hooded, his mouth a hard line.

Okay, maybe it would be more impressive if her stomach wasn't cramped with nerves. But with all that intense anger directed at her, she couldn't help but take a step back. Or glance around for a means of escape.

But, she wasn't really afraid of Jack. More like, cautious. She'd been around men who enjoyed inflicting pain on women, men like her stepfather who only felt powerful and strong when they were beating on someone weaker than themselves. Glenn had hid behind his badge, used his position as a cop to keep from having to pay for all the times he terrorized her family.

Until Dillon had stopped him forever.

And though Jack had the badge, and the ability to crush her like a bug, she didn't believe he'd actually hurt her.

But that didn't mean she was dumb enough to push her luck.

"Look, I'm sorry, all right? I'm just…" She slapped the folded paper against her thigh. "I'm freaked out about all of this. First I read that piece of garbage article, then I went to see Dillon and—"

She stopped abruptly and snapped her mouth shut.

"He what?" Jack asked as he towered over her. He smelled like fresh air and clean sweat. Not a bad combination all in all. "He brushed you off again?"

"Not exactly."

His gaze shifted to somewhere beyond her right shoulder before he met her eyes. "But you did talk to him this morning?"

She squinted up at him. It was an age-old dilemma. Truth or lie? While she tried to be as honest as possible nowadays, she had no problem with lying when the situation called for it. But, since Jack could easily find out the truth on his own, she didn't have much choice.

"He wasn't at his apartment." Jack cursed and took off down the sidewalk toward Sweet Suggestions. "He could be anywhere," Kelsey called as she chased after him.

He turned into the alleyway beside the bakery. "Such as?"

"Well, he could be working."

"It's Sunday."

"Maybe he went out for breakfast. Or he ran out to pick up some milk. There's no reason to go ballistic."

"Since your brother was already in prison," Jack said as he took the steps that led up to Dillon's apartment two at a time, "and more than likely not eager to go back, he's a flight risk."

"So what are you going to do?" she asked from behind him. "Follow his every move? It's a waste of your time. My brother is innocent."

He pounded on the door. "Until that's proven, I'll just keep an eye on him."

"Will you stop that?" She pushed her way between him and the door. "He's not home."

He looked down at her, the expression on his face one of a very frustrated male. "You're in my way."

She crossed her arms. "Good."

He jammed his fingers through his short hair. "What are you doing back here, anyway? I thought you'd left."

Her heart stuttered. He'd thought about her? "How'd you know I'd left?"

"Small town, remember? Word gets around."

"I had to take care of a few things."

He continued to stare at her. The blue of his eyes against his golden skin and the day's worth of dark stubble on his face made him look all the more sexy. All the more dangerous.

Yeah, right. As if she hadn't already figured out he was dangerous. And not just because he wanted to send her brother to prison. Not even because he was a cop and she couldn't trust him.

Any man who kissed like he did was dangerous.

"What are you hoping to accomplish?" he asked.

"I'm here for my brother. To make sure he doesn't go to prison for a crime he didn't commit."

"You mean, unlike the last time he went to prison? When he killed your stepfather?"

She narrowed her eyes. "Low blow, Sheriff."

His gaze dropped to her mouth. The air between them seemed to heat and thicken.

Jack broke the spell with a low curse. He stepped back. "You listen to me and listen good. I have a job to do and people to protect and I won't apologize for it. I sure as hell won't let you or anyone else get in my way. I'll do my job and you can bet your sweet ass I'll do it fairly. But if I find enough evidence to link your brother to Shannon's murder, I will haul him in. Then I'll do everything in my power to make sure he spends the rest of his life in prison."

It wasn't the tone of his voice, or even his words that made her believe he would do just that. It was the determination in his eyes.

"Well, now that I know where you stand, let me fill you in on where I stand." She dropped her arms. "I'm not going anywhere. I will do everything in *my* power to make sure my brother is cleared. And if that means I have to get in your way, then so be it."

"Don't mess with me, Kelsey," he warned softly, and a shiver crept up her spine. "Or this investigation."

Jack turned and stomped down the stairs. Kelsey exhaled heavily, leaned back against the door, and hoped like hell she knew what she was doing by taking on the likes of Jack Martin.

THE TENSION IN KELSEY'S shoulders eased when she walked into the apartment above The Summit and saw Dillon working at the far end of the small kitchen. Thank God. As soon as Jack left Dillon's apartment, she'd jumped in her car to search for her brother. Luckily, her first instinct had been on target.

His back to Kelsey, Dillon screwed large pieces of off-white drywall to the studded walls. Allie stood next to him, her hands on her hips, a frown on her beautiful face. When the drywall was attached, Dillon bent down to pick more screws out of a bucket at his feet.

"Quit being so stubborn," Allie said, tucking her long, dark hair behind her ear. "I want to help."

Before Dillon could respond, Kelsey asked, "Help what?" Allie and Dillon turned simultaneously to face her.

When neither one of them said anything, Kelsey walked farther into the room. "What's going on?"

While Dillon remained silent, Allie rolled her eyes. "I'm an attorney. Or was, before I quit my job to run this place." She wrinkled her nose. "Technically, I guess I still am an attorney. I mean, I passed the bar—not this bar, the legal bar—and just because I'm not—"

"Allie," Dillon interrupted with a hint of humor in his voice, his lips turned up at the corners.

Kelsey blinked. The fondness in Dillon's expression as he looked at Allie made Kelsey feel odd. She could remember when he used to look at her with the same mixture of exasperation and affection.

Damn it, all she wanted was her brother back in her life, the way they used to be before she'd royally messed up. Was that too much to ask for?

"Anyway," Allie continued. "I'm still an attorney, just not a practicing one. But I can change that if you need my help," she said, turning to face Dillon.

"I appreciate the offer, but I don't want you involved." He crossed to the corner of the room and pulled a piece of drywall off the pile. "Besides, I don't need a lawyer."

"Why aren't you doing anything to help your cause?" Kelsey asked, unable to keep the frustration out of her voice.

"Whatever happens, happens. I can't control it."

"You might not be able to control it, but I'll be damned if I'm going to sit around and let you take the fall for something you didn't do."

He leaned the drywall against the wall. "You really have no say in the matter."

Allie laid her hand on Dillon's arm. Either in silent support or a reprimand, Kelsey wasn't sure which. Either way, the easy familiarity between Allie and Dillon—and the fact that Dillon didn't seem to hate Allie's guts—upset her.

"If Allie's willing to help, I think you should consider her offer."

He grunted as he lifted the drywall into place. "Not interested."

At his indifferent tone she forgot all about remaining calm. "Well, maybe you should be interested," Kelsey said over the high-pitched whine of the drill. "Seeing as how you were publicly found guilty in the newspaper today—"

"They can't convict me because of a newspaper article."

"—and now the cops think you've run off. They've probably already put out an APB or whatever it is they put out when someone's missing. Which means you're three-quarters of the way to being totally screwed."

Dillon stopped drilling and sent her a narrow look over his shoulder. "What the hell are you talking about?"

Damn. Her and her big mouth. She shrugged and attempted to look less guilty than she felt. Not easy.

"I went by your apartment earlier and you weren't there," she admitted.

"And?"

"And…I sort of ran into the chief of police and sort of told him you weren't home."

His jaw twitched as if he were gritting his teeth. "And now Chief Martin thinks I've left town?"

"Something like that," she muttered.

"You never cease to amaze me."

Somehow she didn't think he meant that as a compliment. "Yeah, well. I try." Kelsey stuck her hands in her front pockets. "The way Jack freaked out—"

"Jack?" Dillon's expression hardened. "What's this? You cozying up to a cop?"

Her face warmed. "The way he acted, gave me the impression you were more than just a person of interest in this case."

"No kidding." He turned back to his work and screwed another screw into the drywall. "I'm more of a prime suspect. Which is why I don't want Allie involved. Not only is her brother investigating me, but she's trying to get a business up and running. I don't want to risk her reputation being tarnished. And I don't want you involved, either."

"Too late," Kelsey said.

Dillon spun around. "Why are you even still here?"

She fought the urge to touch him, to lay her hand on his arm like Allie had done, to connect with him on some small level.

"You know why." She spoke the words softly, honestly. And hoped he'd finally give her a second chance. "You saved my life—"

"I killed a man," he stated flatly. "I don't want you to repay me for that."

When he turned his back on Kelsey again, Allie stepped between them. She glanced at Dillon's rigid back. "I uh, heard about you getting the boot at The Bee Hive, Kelsey."

That revelation made Dillon whirl to face her again. Jeez, at this rate the guy was one fast spin away from whiplash.

Kelsey fidgeted, realized she was fidgeting and forced herself to stand still. "News sure travels fast here."

"No doubt about that," Allie said.

"It's no big deal."

"You were kicked out of the B and B?" Dillon asked. "It's a sign you need to get out of this town. It'll only get worse. No one in town is going to rent you a room. Not if they know you're connected to me."

"I'll be fine."

"How? By sleeping in your car?"

She hesitated. "I could…stay with you."

His mouth thinned. "No."

"She can crash up here," Allie said quickly. She smiled at Kelsey. "If you don't mind the mess or living above a bar."

And wouldn't that go over well with the sexy police chief? "Thanks for the offer—"

"Yeah," Dillon said darkly. "Thanks a lot."

Allie grinned. Patted Dillon's cheek. "No problem."

"But I'm not sure that would be a good idea," Kelsey hedged.

Allie tilted her head to the side. "Why not?"

"Your brother's not too happy with me at the moment." She remembered how angry Jack had been when he'd told her to stay out of his way. "I don't want to make things worse than they are."

Dillon groaned. "Don't tell me you've only been in town less than three days and you've already pissed off the police chief?"

"It didn't take much. He's pretty easy to piss off."

"Are we talking about the same guy?" Allie asked. "My big brother, Jack Martin? The poster boy for the strong and silent type?"

Kelsey shrugged and nudged the box of screws with her toe. "It must just be me, then." Which was disappointing, but not surprising.

"When will you learn you can't go around antagonizing people?" Dillon asked, his voice laced with frustration. "Especially people in certain positions."

"Jack would never use his position as police chief for his own personal gain," Allie said, defending her brother.

Kelsey wanted to agree, but kept her opinion to herself when she saw that Dillon obviously didn't share the same thought. They both knew what happened when cops abused their power and connections. It was part of the reason Dillon had been found guilty of manslaughter instead of being let go for killing Glenn out of self-defense.

"Doesn't matter," Dillon insisted. "Haven't you grown up at all?"

His words hit her like a slap. "I wasn't trying to—"

"You never do." His aggravation and disappointment made her heart ache. "You want to help me? Steer clear of the police. Better yet, stay away from me. And for God's sake, don't do anything else to piss off Jack Martin."

He went back to his work. Kelsey turned away. It hurt to

know he was upset with her, that he still thought of her as the troublemaker she'd been all those years ago.

Damn it, she had changed.

And she would prove it.

CHAPTER SIX

HE WAS MISSING SOMETHING. Jack sipped his coffee and studied the hand-drawn map of Edgewood Lane he'd pinned onto Shannon's murder board. There were only four buildings on the secluded, dead-end road on the outskirts of town. At the beginning of the lane was the Crandall house, across from it the Schuman residence. Mayor Christine Michaels and her only child, Ben, lived at the end of the lane. The fourth structure was the Michaels's large horse stable that sat halfway between their home and the Crandalls', approximately one hundred yards from each house.

He rubbed his free hand over his stomach as he reread his notes. Something nagged at him, niggled at the edge of his brain. A piece of the puzzle just didn't fit. When it did slip into place, would it prove Ward's guilt? Or innocence?

A knock at the door was followed by a soft voice. "Jack? Do you have a minute?"

Jack quickly covered the board with a blanket he'd snatched from the supply closet and then turned to face Mayor Michaels.

Her straight, shoulder-length brown hair was streaked gold from spending so much time outdoors and her skin still held the faintest trace of summer bronze. The white blouse she wore beneath her conservative black jacket was buttoned almost to her chin while her black skirt reached her ankles. The high heels of her pumps brought her height to just under six feet.

Despite her Sunday-school-teacher appearance, Jack knew Mayor Michaels was ambitious, politically savvy and a force to be reckoned with.

"Of course," Jack said as he took the seat behind his desk. "What can I do for you?"

Christine closed the door behind her and crossed the small room to him, bringing with her the subtle scent of hay and horses. "How close are you to arresting Dillon Ward for Shannon's murder?"

He slowly set his coffee cup down on his desk. "I'm in the process of gathering information—"

"Do you really need more information?" Christine sat down and leaned forward. Placed the newspaper onto his desk. "According to this article, you have ample reason to arrest Ward for the murder now."

That damn article again. He'd already spent the better part of an hour on the phone reaming Dora up one side and down the other. Not that it had fazed Serenity Springs's intrepid editor in chief any. After the fifth time Dora quoted the first amendment—word for word—Jack had hung up the phone.

"Well?" Mayor Michaels linked her large hands together on his desk, a frown wrinkling her forehead. "Is Dora's article true?"

"The facts are true," he conceded carefully, "but it's not only what I need, it's also what the district attorney's office needs. There isn't enough to hold Ward. Not yet."

"But Dillon Ward admitted he went home with Shannon.

By all accounts, he's the last person to have seen her alive. You even have a witness who saw him there."

"Carla Schuman saw his truck there, that's all." Unfortunately, Carla hadn't noticed what time Ward had left Shannon's. Neither had her husband or teenage daughter. "Ward claims he went to her house to get the money she owed him for laying the tile floor in her bathroom."

The mayor studied him. "You believe him?"

"What I believe or don't believe is irrelevant. It's what I can prove that's important."

At the moment, he couldn't prove a hell of a lot. Yes, Ward admitted he'd been at Shannon's house and that they'd argued when, instead of paying him what she owed, Shannon came on to him. According to Ward, once he'd told her he wasn't interested, Shannon freaked and kicked him out.

"Far be it from me to tell you how to do your job," Christine said, her tone making it clear that while she may not like telling him what to do, that wasn't going to stop her. "But you may want to get your proof and get this case solved. There are a lot of people in town who want Ward arrested. The sooner, the better."

"If Dillon Ward is guilty, I'll do everything in my power to bring him to justice. I'm sure the last thing you, or anyone in town wants is for me to jeopardize the state's case by arresting him too soon."

"Are you sure that's the only reason?"

Though his neck muscles tightened, Jack kept his expression neutral. "Meaning?"

"There have been certain…rumors about Dillon Ward." She paused, either because she was unsure of how much to say or, more than likely, for dramatic effect. "And your sister."

"There are always rumors floating around," he said mildly.

She nodded. "That's true, but I think, in this case, it would be in everyone's best interest if Dillon Ward wasn't associating with your sister, don't you?"

"I don't choose Allie's associates."

"The prime suspect in a murder case working for the police chief's sister?" She sighed. "I hate to say it, Jack, but it's a clear conflict of interest."

"What would you have me do?"

"Maybe we should let the state police take over."

Hell. "You want to pull us off this case?"

"It's not what I want, it's what city council is suggesting. Mark Crandall specifically."

Jack finished his coffee. "I understand how Mark feels, but rushing to make an arrest without enough proof for a conviction, isn't going to do anyone any good."

Christine sat back. "You can't blame the man for being upset. His wife was murdered and the main suspect is walking the streets. Jack, the citizens of this town want to know their police department is doing all it can to protect them. They want a police department they can trust, one that'll make the right decisions and won't jeopardize their safety."

Jack narrowed his eyes and wondered if that was a not-so-subtle reference to the mistake he'd made three years ago while still with the NYPD. "The state police are providing valuable services and expertise—with the Serenity Springs PD's full cooperation and gratitude—but that's all."

Christine stood. "I was hoping it wouldn't come to this, but if you don't get the proof you need to arrest Dillon Ward…"

"What?" he asked softly, struggling to keep his temper in check.

She straightened her shoulders. "If you don't get the proof you need, city council is making noises about removing you as chief of police."

Jack pressed his lips together. This was turning into one big nightmare. "City council hired me to do a job, a job I've done well. And while I understand both Mark Crandall's and the council's positions, I won't stand by while they hand over this investigation to another department."

"This isn't personal, Jack. But you should know, if it comes down to it and I have to step in to make sure this investigation is run the right way, you might not have a choice."

"Personal or not, you can tell the council I'm going to run this investigation *my* way. By the book. Honestly. Fairly." He kept his voice even, reminding himself that the mayor was the messenger, not, as far as he could tell, the instigator in this mess. "If anyone has a problem with my job performance, they can very well try and get me fired. Until then, I'm in charge and I won't allow anyone, not even you, to interfere."

"I'm on your side," Christine said, her admission surprising him. For the past six years the mayor had made a career out of not choosing sides. "Just let me give you some friendly advice. Be careful. I'm afraid this isn't over."

Damn right it wasn't over, he thought as the mayor left his office, shutting the door with a soft click. Jack knew it was only the beginning.

SERENITY SPRINGS'S BIG, BAD police chief lived in a small, bricked Cape Cod with twin front gables and arched windows. Three miles from downtown and surrounded by woods, it was well maintained, charming and so cute, it made Kelsey's teeth ache.

She slipped her purse off her left shoulder and onto her right. Okay, she'd come this far, no turning back now.

Smoothing a hand over her hair, she climbed stone steps in the middle of a grassy hill. A strong gust of wind blew, and though she couldn't see them, she could hear the rustling of leaves.

She reached the covered porch and took a shaky breath. The cool, fresh air tickled her nose as she filled her lungs. There was one reason, and one reason only why she was at Jack's house at nine o'clock on a Sunday night.

To grovel.

She made a face. She was not looking forward to this. But Dillon was so upset with her that she'd decided she needed to make nice with the cop.

If begging Jack's forgiveness didn't prove she'd do anything to help her brother, and that she'd changed, nothing would.

Of course, just because she apologized didn't mean Jack had to forgive her.

She wiped a damp palm down the front of her denim miniskirt. Okay, so she'd given into her vanity by dressing up somewhat. Her skirt hugged her hips and redefined the word *short*. The strappy sandals she wore added three inches to her height, and her dark-green top clung to her breasts and bared her belly-button ring. She'd even put on a bit of makeup. Nothing much, just a hint of mascara, light blusher and lip gloss.

She pounded a bit harder on the door than necessary. The porch light came on and the door swung open. And there he was, in all his six-foot glory. She drew in a deep breath. God, he smelled good. Like musky aftershave and…chocolate?

"This isn't a good time," Jack said.

She tilted her head to the side and studied him. He hadn't shaved and the stubble that had covered his chin that morning was now thick and dark. She would have liked to rub her cheek against his just to feel the scrape of his whiskers. Over his jeans and T-shirt he wore a stained white apron with the words *Dressed to Grill* scrolled across in red print.

From the top of his mussed hair to the tips of his bare feet, he looked hot, flustered and good enough to eat.

"This won't take long," she said, praying it was the truth. How long could humiliating oneself take?

He glanced behind him before focusing on her again. "Well? What is it?"

She reminded herself why she was there, and bit back the smart-ass rejoinder that sprang to her lips. "I just wanted to say…this morning when we ran into each other, I might have been a bit…"

She trailed off when Jack glanced behind him once again. Frowning, she attempted to look beyond him into the house but he moved and blocked her view.

"What is wrong with you?" she asked.

"Nothing," he said and stepped fully onto the porch, leaving the door opened a crack behind him.

Her stomach churned. He must not be alone. Why else would he be so nervous, looking over his shoulder like that, keeping his voice down?

She could easily imagine the type of woman Jack went for. She'd be blond with long, wavy hair, big blue eyes and curves to spare. And, seeing as how he'd turned down Shannon Crandall the other night, he probably preferred his blondes less obvious and more…perky.

Oh, man, perky blondes were definitely worse than air-headed blondes, buxom blondes or even bleached blondes. Perky ones were always so damn friendly.

Not that it bothered Kelsey or anything. She was only interested in Jack because he held her brother's life in his hands. She didn't care who he was with or what he did with his personal life.

"You jerk," she spat and slapped him on the arm. She attempted to storm off but he grabbed her by the elbow and jerked her around to face him.

"What the hell was that for?" he demanded.

She tugged on her arm, but he refused to release her. "Let go."

He looked down at his hand, then dragged it down her arm. The callused tips of his fingers grazed her wrist, sending her pulse skittering.

He finally stepped back, dropping his hand to his side. With no little amount of effort, she fisted her tingling fingers into her palm.

"You do realize you just assaulted a police officer, don't you?"

"I didn't hit you because you're a cop. I hit you because you're a man."

He shook his head. "Care to elaborate?"

"No." Hands on her hips, she tapped her toe several times. "But for the record, I don't like the idea of you trying to sleep with me if you have a girlfriend."

"What?" She saw realization dawn in his eyes. He glanced over his shoulder before leaning toward her. "Is this about the other night? Because even though it was a mistake and never should have happened, I'm not involved with anyone."

He straightened. "And I didn't try to sleep with you. It was just a kiss."

Because it was the truth she mumbled, "It was a great kiss."

He shrugged as if it didn't matter but she could see in his eyes that he agreed.

"But you're right," she admitted grudgingly. "It was only a kiss. Good thing, too. With all this other stuff going on, a sexual relationship between us would be too…complicated."

An unexpected, sexy grin lit his face. "Honey, if we were to have sex, I promise you complications wouldn't even cross your mind."

She blinked. "Conceited, aren't you?"

"Confident."

Oh, she had no doubt he'd be good at it. Someone with his looks was bound to know a thing or two. Plus, they'd had that kiss. *Very* nice.

But she needed to remember who she was dealing with here. Jack was a cop first. And, while all signs pointed to him being one of the good guys, she was afraid that might just be wishful thinking on her part. Even though he claimed he wasn't involved with anyone, he was still acting weird.

"I'll let you get back to your evening," she said and stepped back. She needed to get out of there before she made a bigger ass of herself. If that was even possible.

"Kelsey…"

That's all he said. Just her name. But the sound of it, rolling off his tongue in his husky voice, was enough to stop her.

"I'm glad you stopped by and that you realize that kiss was a mistake."

Since there was no way she could force words past the stupid lump in her throat, she simply nodded. Yeah, a mistake. One she was having a hard time regretting.

"The beeper thingy just went off."

Kelsey jerked her head up at the soft voice coming from behind Jack. Through the buzzing in her head she heard Jack muttering but couldn't make out the words. The only clear thought she had was that she'd been right.

He had a female in the house. And that female had dark-blond hair, blue eyes and was wearing purple pajamas with cartoon frogs on them. She didn't have a curvaceous body though. At least not yet.

The mystery woman was a child.

"Daddy," the kid said, tugging on Jack's apron. "Did you hear me? The cookies are gonna burn."

Daddy? Kelsey's eyes flew to Jack. He smiled down at the kid and ruffled her hair.

Kelsey swallowed. Holy God.

Jack was a daddy.

JACK DIDN'T KNOW WHAT to make of Kelsey's obviously shocked reaction to Emma.

"Come on, squirt," he said to his daughter who was staring up at Kelsey with undisguised curiosity. "Let's go get those cookies."

He didn't wait to see if Emma followed, just bolted for his kitchen. He took the cookies out and set them on top of the stove. After tossing the oven mitt on the table, he raced back to the porch in record time.

And arrived just as his sweet, precocious daughter told Kelsey, "You have hair like a boy's."

Jack groaned. His kid was smart as a whip, but she needed to brush up on her manners.

"Emma," he said, using his stern dad voice, "that's not polite."

Her little forehead wrinkled. "It's not?"

"No."

"That's okay." Kelsey's voice seemed strained as she lifted a hand and touched her hair self-consciously. "It is short like a boy's. I like it short."

"Oh." Emma tipped her head back and squinted up at Kelsey. "And it's a funny color."

"Em-ma." That was it. Maybe he should do something. Like wash her mouth out.

And he would. As soon as they made a nontoxic, candy flavored soap.

Kelsey had a definite deer-in-the-headlights look about her. "Uh, well, my mom had red hair."

"My mommy had yellow hair, like mine. She's in heaven." Emma tugged on Kelsey's skirt. "Is your mommy in heaven?"

"No. My mom is most definitely not in heaven."

Before he could stop her, Emma reached out and poked Kelsey's stomach with her finger. "I can see your belly button."

To his amazement, Kelsey blushed. He grabbed Emma and scooted her away from Kelsey's stomach. Although now that Emma mentioned it, he couldn't help but take a quick peek.

Uh-huh. Like he hadn't already noticed that Kelsey's shirt stopped a few inches above the waist of her skirt revealing a tantalizing glimpse of smooth, pale flesh and a glittery belly-button ring.

He also hadn't missed the amount of leg on display in her

short skirt. The images would probably torture him with yet another restless, sweat-soaked night.

Terrific.

"I, uh…" Kelsey tugged her shirt down. Luckily for him, it refused to stay put. "I guess you can."

"Britney Spears shows her belly button. But Daddy says I'm not allowed."

"Well," Kelsey said and damn if her voice didn't sound panicked, "that's, uh, good advice."

Emma shrugged one shoulder.

Kelsey's eyes kept darting back to the sidewalk, as if judging if it was safe to make a run for it. At first he'd wondered if Emma had actually hurt her feelings, remarking on her hair that way. But now—it sounded crazy—but he wondered if Kelsey was nervous.

His six-year-old daughter made her nervous.

Wasn't that interesting?

"Did they hurt? You have lots of earrings," Emma explained when Kelsey just stared. "And one in your belly button. Did they hurt?"

"Only for a minute. It feels like a shot, you know, when you go to the doctor."

"I had to get three shots before kindergarten." She looked up at him. "But I didn't cry, did I, Daddy?"

"No, you didn't. You were very brave."

"Hayley has her ears pierced." Emma fingered her own hole-less earlobes. "She got them for her sixth birthday."

"Oh, well, that's, uh—"

"I got a Bratz doll," Emma said pitifully. As if she hadn't pestered him for two months straight to get her one.

Kelsey's startled gaze met his. "They name dolls after brats?"

He cleared his throat. Tried not to think about how good she smelled. "Bratz. With a *z*."

"Daddy won't let me get my ears pierced," Emma said, sliding him a petulant look.

"I didn't say you couldn't get your ears pierced." Ear-piercing conversation number two hundred and eleven coming right up. "I said you were too young to get them pierced now."

"When can I, Daddy?"

"When you've graduated from college."

Emma stuck her lower lip out. "Daddy."

Jack noticed Kelsey looking back and forth between them. Who would have thought that all it would take for calm, cool and cocky Kelsey to be rendered speechless was a child?

"Well," Kelsey said, already taking a step backward. "I should probably be—"

"Do you want to help us make cookies?" Emma grabbed her hand and began tugging her into the house. "It's my turn to bring them for snack tomorrow."

"Oh, I don't think so," Kelsey said at the same time Jack blurted out, "No!"

Both Kelsey and Emma looked at him wide-eyed. He cleared his throat, forced a smile. "I mean, I'm sure Kelsey's busy. Besides, the cookies are all done."

"You can come in and eat a cookie, then," Emma said. "Please. Can she please stay, Daddy?"

Emma clasped her hands together and sent him the pleading look little girls have used on their daddies for centuries. It was like a father's kryptonite.

Never had it been more important to resist that look than at that moment. Because he knew what his daughter was thinking, knew what she was hoping.

He knew how badly Emma wanted a mother. Any woman would do. The nice lady at the grocery store who smiled at her. The barely legal girl who waited on them at the Snow Pine Restaurant. And her favorite of them all, Nina Carlson. Not only did Nina own Sweet Suggestions, but she could bake, was blond and had two kids of her own.

So there was no way he could allow Kelsey around his daughter. It was also why, when he was involved with a woman, he kept the relationship casual. And he never brought a woman he was seeing to his home or introduced her to his daughter.

And with Kelsey's brother as a prime suspect in his murder investigation, any relationship with her—no matter how innocent—would cause problems. For all of them.

"Honey," he said, "Kelsey has to go."

"Then I'll go get her a cookie, okay?" She ran into the house, yelled over her shoulder, "I'll be right back. Don't go anywhere."

"Take one that's already cool," Jack called.

"So," she said. "You have a daughter."

"Yeah."

He leaned back and waited. Most women couldn't say enough about Emma. How pretty she was. How smart. Which, of course, he already knew. But he never got tired of hearing it.

"She's…uh…something."

He narrowed his eyes. What the hell did that mean?

Before he could demand an explanation, Kelsey added, "Look, I really don't need a cookie. Why don't I—"

"Here you go," Emma called cheerfully as she reappeared with a flat cookie in her small hand.

"Uh, thanks." Kelsey eyed the cookie more warily than necessary if you'd have asked him. "Uh, I'll just have a bite."

She broke a piece off and…man, she actually sniffed it. After taking a deep breath, she popped the crumb into her mouth.

Emma's eyes shone as she watched her. But he didn't miss Kelsey's grimace.

She chewed, swallowed and looked at Jack. "Could I talk to you for a minute?"

He shrugged and moved farther out onto the porch, well aware of his daughter's curiosity.

"I hate to tell you this," she said, her voice so low he had to bend close to hear her. "Seeing as how you're dressed to grill and all, but your cookies—" She stopped, cleared her throat.

"What about them?"

"Well, they're…"

Jack whipped around at the sounds of gagging and retching. He knelt by Emma. "What's wrong? Are you sick?"

Emma, her face squinched up in disgust, spat chewed cookie onto the porch and threw the remains over the rail into the grass. "These cookies are yucky, Daddy!"

And with Kelsey as a witness, his daughter promptly burst into tears.

CHAPTER SEVEN

KELSEY SHIVERED IN THE COOL breeze. But that didn't stop a bead of perspiration from trickling down her back. Kids did that to her. Made her sweat.

Jack was kneeling in front of his daughter and Kelsey squeezed her eyes shut. His daughter. Talk about a surprise. It had never crossed her mind that Jack could be a father.

Not that it should have. It wasn't like they'd known each other all that long. Or had many meaningful discussions. She knew he was a cop and intent on sending her brother to prison, but that was all.

Which she probably should've considered two nights ago when they'd kissed.

Okay, so her hormones had taken over. Heat of the moment and all that—still, it didn't fully excuse her actions. For God's sake, she'd kissed a cop. And not just any cop but the chief of police, who also happened to be a single father.

It was like the end of the world as she knew it.

Jack picked up Emma and murmured to the little girl in an attempt to get her to stop crying. He kissed her tear-stained cheek and rubbed slow circles over her back.

Kelsey's mouth went dry. There was definitely something wrong with her. Why else would she be thinking about the way Jack had kissed *her* the other night? About how it had felt when his large hand had slipped under her shirt and caressed her skin.

"Take it easy," Jack said. "They can't be that bad."

Kelsey blinked. He wasn't even talking to her. He was talking to Emma. Emma whose eyes glimmered with tears, an occasional, soft hiccup escaping her Kewpie doll mouth. Emma who stared up at him with all the love and adoration little girls are supposed to feel for their daddies.

Kelsey's heart contracted. The connection between Jack and his daughter, the way he attempted to soothe her, was so pure and sweet. For the first time in years Kelsey regretted what she'd never had. Her own father took off before she was born but growing up she'd told herself she didn't miss not having a dad. And yet, when her mother married Glenn Hopkins, she'd been stupid enough to hope that Glenn could be the father she'd always pretended she never wanted.

Those hopes were effectively killed a short time later when Glenn split her lip for not cleaning her room.

Admittedly, she didn't know much about raising kids, or even what it was like to be a daughter who gazed up at her father with absolute trust and complete, unabashed love. But jeez, Emma was looking at Jack like he was the Tooth Fairy, Easter Bunny and Santa Claus all rolled into one.

Well, technically he was all those things. And he was trying to pull a fast one over on Emma. Which made his duplicity even worse. Santa would just admit the cookies were awful and move on from there.

It was up to her to set him straight.

"Oh, they are," Kelsey assured him. After all, she'd had the bad luck of tasting one. "Those cookies are really, really bad."

Emma's lower lip quivered before she sent up a wail that had the hair on the back of Kelsey's neck standing on end.

Jack patted Emma's back. "I'm…sure…they're…fine." He grit out the words over the kid's cries.

Right. Like saying it slowly and stressing the word *fine* is going to somehow transform a bunch of toxic cookies into something edible. Good plan.

Kelsey shrugged. It was no skin off hers if Jack sent his daughter to school with bad cookies.

A sudden vision of a roomful of little kids clutching their stomachs and writhing on the floor in agony assaulted her.

"Look," she said, "I know you don't want to hear this, but I can't stand by and say nothing. It would be cruel."

Jack frowned at her over Emma's head. "Don't you think you're being a tad overdramatic?"

His kid was blubbering away, shaking her head back and forth in a display of angst the likes of which Kelsey had never seen. And he thought she was overly dramatic?

"No. I don't." Could he at least tell Emma to tone it down? But Jack just continued with the useless jiggling and back patting. Kelsey raised her voice. "Have you tried one?"

"No, but I'm—"

"Hey, kid," Kelsey said, and Emma turned to her in surprise. "Suck it up already… You can stop crying now."

A muscle jumped in Jack's jaw. "Don't yell at my daughter."

"That wasn't yelling." She should know. Growing up, if Glenn wasn't using his fists, he was yelling.

Amazingly, Emma stopped crying.

Not knowing how long this reprieve would last, she ignored Jack's anger and kept her gaze on Emma. "Why don't you go get your daddy one of those cookies? Let him decide for himself how they taste."

Emma sniffed and used her sleeve to wipe her nose, making Kelsey grimace. "Okay," she said with another sniff and wiggled until Jack set her down.

"Listen," he said when Emma was out of earshot, "I'm sure the cookies aren't that bad. And I don't appreciate you upsetting Emma."

"Yeah, well, I'm betting the other parents aren't going to appreciate their kids having their stomachs pumped."

He drew closer to her. "I made those cookies myself."

"I wouldn't brag about it if I were you."

He was so close now, her fingers twitched with the need to touch him. She attempted to push back the growing awareness, the building desire. But she made the mistake of looking up into his gorgeous blue eyes. All thoughts emptied from her head as her heart picked up speed. Her body yearned to close the distance separating them.

Emma burst through the doorway and Kelsey took a quick step back.

"Here, Daddy." Emma pushed between Jack and Kelsey and held a cookie up to him. "Try it."

Jack smiled down at his daughter and shoved the entire cookie into his mouth.

That wasn't a smart move. Having been on the receiving end of those cookies, Kelsey felt for him. But that didn't stop her from smirking.

His face remained expressionless as he chewed. And chewed. And chewed. He swallowed mightily.

She didn't bother to conceal her triumphant expression. Just tilted her head, grinned sweetly and asked, "Want another?"

JACK FOUGHT THE GAG REFLEX. "No, thanks. You made your point." He knelt back down to face Emma, steeling himself against the tears he knew would come. "Listen, honey, why don't we forget about the cookies? We can call Nina and—"

And just like that, Emma's eyes filled up again.

"Hey, it's all right." He gathered her close. "We'll stop by Sweet Suggestions in the morning—"

"No!" Emma sobbed.

"Why not? We'll pick up something better than regular cookies. How about those cupcakes you like? The ones with the sprinkles?"

"I don't want to buy cupcakes," Emma insisted. In the circle of his arms her body was stiff and unyielding, her face red and wet from tears. "I told all the kids we were gonna make cookies."

He bit back a frustrated sigh. "They won't care, honey. And once they see the cupcakes they'll—"

"They will care. Everyone always brings in cookies. No one buys cupcakes. And Miranda will laugh. She'll laugh and say she told me so."

Jack sat back on his heels. "Miranda? Wasn't she in your kindergarten class?"

Emma nodded, her words coming out choppy. "She says… I'm the only one…who doesn't have a mmm…mommy to make cookies with me. And…I told her that I had a…a daddy and that we could so make cookies." Her face scrunched up again. "But she said…she said…daddies weren't like mommies. She said daddies can't make cookies."

He felt sick. "You tell her…" He stopped and thought better of what he'd been about to say. "Listen to me, Emma. Here…" He wiped her tears gently away with his fingertips.

"Are you listening?" He waited until she nodded. "Good. It doesn't matter what Miranda says. Daddies can too make cookies, and the next time it's your turn to bring in a snack, we'll make the best cookies ever. I promise."

Emma's breath quivered out softly. The knot in his gut loosened. He couldn't believe it. He'd managed to get through to her.

"I want to make them now," Emma said, fresh tears falling.

He closed his eyes and wondered if it was too late in the parenting game to ask for operating instructions. "Hey, squirt, why don't you run inside and throw all those cookies in the garbage?"

"But, Daddy—"

Jack straightened, laid his hand on her head. "Go blow your nose and wipe all those tears away," he said using his best cop voice. When in doubt, revert to what you know. "We'll figure something out."

Of course his cop voice had no effect on Emma. She didn't budge. "You promise, Daddy?"

"I promise," Jack said solemnly. He gave her a slight swat on the behind and, well aware of Kelsey's attention on their byplay, prayed Emma would do as she was told.

He watched in relief as his daughter ran into the house. Now if he could just leap tall buildings in a single bound, he'd be all set.

"Your cookies sucked," Kelsey said into the silence, "but you did a good job with her."

He didn't care what Kelsey thought of him. Couldn't afford to care. Her opinions about him, his job—specifically the way he handled Shannon's murder case—or his parenting skills meant nothing.

So why did her praise warm his heart?

"Thanks. Now I have to figure out what I'm going to do. To make more cookies I'll have to run to the store." He held his watch up to his face, swore softly. "The store that closed four hours ago."

"What do you need?"

"Chocolate chips. Eggs. And some baking soda."

"You ran out of all those with that last batch?"

"Not exactly."

"You didn't follow the recipe, did you?"

"I followed the recipe." He wasn't a complete moron. "I just didn't have any baking soda. Or eggs. And since I didn't have any chocolate chips, I broke up a couple of chocolate bars."

"Why did you go to all the trouble of making cookies when you didn't have all the ingredients?" she asked, and he could've sworn he heard a smile in her voice.

"I didn't think it would matter."

"Uh...wrong."

"Cut me some slack. I wasn't planning on playing Betty Crocker tonight." Not until he'd discovered the note in Emma's backpack reminding him it was her turn to bring in a snack for school tomorrow.

Kelsey stepped toward him, back under the light. "What's the big deal? Just buy the cupcakes. The kid'll get over it."

He rubbed a hand over his face. Damn, but he was tired. "I doubt it."

"Why?"

He pressed his lips together. "Let's just say the last time it was her turn to bring in a snack, I sort of dropped the ball."

She raised her eyebrows. "Oh, now this I have to hear."

"It's no big deal. I didn't find the note reminding me it was our turn until we were walking out the door and…" He shook his head. "It doesn't matter."

"Come on. What did you send with her? Granola bars? Carrot sticks? Low-fat muffins?"

"Raisin bran," he mumbled.

"What?"

"I sent in twenty-two sandwich bags of raisin bran."

Her low, husky laughter sent a ripple of awareness up his spine. "Oh, man. You *so* owe her."

"I know. But I'll handle it."

He needed Kelsey gone so he could be left alone to deal with his daughter and this miniature crisis. He tried not to rely on others or ask for help with Emma. And he sure as hell didn't want to start now, not with Kelsey Reagan.

Except Kelsey hadn't moved.

Jack reached behind him and held open the door. "It's getting late," he said, taking a step back. "You probably need to get going."

"Do you have any oatmeal?"

He froze. "Oatmeal?"

"Yes. Not the instant kind, either."

"You want me to give the kids sandwich bags of oatmeal?"

"No," she said in exasperation with a hint of humor. "Do you have any or not?"

"I think so. My mom makes it for Emma for breakfast sometimes—"

"What about sugar? And butter?"

"Yeah…why?"

She sighed deeply. "It looks like I'm going to do you a favor here, Sheriff."

God help him, even with his job on the line and his kid crying buckets, he didn't have any problem coming up with what type of favor he'd like Kelsey to do for him. "Don't take this the wrong way, but you don't strike me as a woman who goes around granting *favors*."

"Usually I don't. But here's the deal. I can help save your butt with the kid, help her save face at school and put that little twit Miranda in her place."

Jack knew it was wrong—wrong, spiteful and more than a bit immature—to want to put a six-year-old in her place. So why did it sound like such a good idea to him?

"I'm listening."

"Okay. So, I help you and the kid make cookies—"

"You can make cookies?"

"I'm multitalented," she said dryly.

"What do you want in exchange?"

"Nothing."

He laughed. "Right. You expect me to believe you want to help me and my daughter and want nothing in return?" He shook his head, leaned in closer so he could see her better. "I'm not buying it."

"I'm trying to be nice here and you're not making it easy."

No, he wasn't. "I appreciate the offer," he told her, "but I'm going to pass."

Anger flashed in her eyes. And he wasn't sure, but he thought he detected a trace of hurt as well. "You don't want my help? Fine. But my cookies are a hell of a lot better than—"

"You know how to make cookies?"

Jack groaned. "Emma, I thought I asked you to wait in—"

"Can you stay and help us make cookies?" Emma asked as she slipped past Jack. *"Please? Pretty please?"*

"Kelsey has to go."

"I could probably stick around for a few minutes." She looked down at Emma. "If it's okay with your dad."

"Oh, please, Daddy. *Please!*" Emma grabbed Kelsey's hand and began hopping up and down. "Can she stay and help?"

Knowing he didn't stand a chance, Jack nodded. Emma gave a whoop of delight and pulled Kelsey into his house.

THE KID DIDN'T SHUT UP.

"Now I'm in first grade and my teacher's name is Miss Clark." Emma stood on a chair next to the counter and dropped the last gooey spoonful of chocolate no-bakes onto a sheet of tin foil. "And tomorrow we have gym and we have to do curl ups. I can do twenty."

Kelsey felt her eyes cross. Jeez, she already knew more about the kid than she'd ever thought possible. Emma had talked nonstop since they'd gone inside, filling Kelsey in on her entire life's story. Who would've thought someone who'd only been alive for six years had so much to say?

It had taken a full thirty minutes, but Kelsey had successfully been brought up-to-date on the life and times of Emma Martin.

What more could there be?

Except, hallelujah, the kid finally stopped talking. She glanced over to make sure Emma was still breathing and saw the expectant look on the little girl's face.

"Oh," she said when realization dawned. Emma wanted her to comment about—what had Emma been saying? Oh, yeah. Gym class. Curl ups. "Uh, that's good."

An adorable smile lit Emma's face. Huh. Well what do you

know? She'd said the right thing. Looked like someone deserved a gold star.

"These are yummy," Emma said around a bite of her third cookie. "Did your mommy teach you how to make them?"

Seeing as how there weren't too many cookie recipes that included vodka as a main ingredient, Leigh hadn't done much baking. Or mothering, for that matter.

Not that the kid needed to know that. Emma's life may not be perfect—what with her mother dead and all—but, compared to what Kelsey had survived, it was pretty damn close.

"No, my mother didn't teach me." Jack's arm brushed her back as he squeezed past her. The kitchen was narrow, but warm and comfortable with light wood cabinets, white counters and appliances and a cream-and-green tiled floor. "My brother did."

"You have a brother?" Emma asked in an awed tone. As if she had just admitted to being on a first-name basis with Cinderella or something.

"Yeah. His name is Dillon."

"I want a baby brother. But Daddy won't get me one."

Kelsey's lips twitched and she couldn't stop herself from looking over at the sink where Jack washed dishes, his face a cool mask. He hadn't said much while she'd helped Emma with the no-bakes, but it was obvious he wasn't happy with her being in his house or helping his kid.

So much for not pissing him off anymore.

"Well," Kelsey said, tearing her gaze away from Jack—who knew a man doing domestic chores could be so sexy? "Dillon's older than me."

Emma frowned. "I don't want an older brother. Hayley says older brothers are a pain in the butt."

"Language," Jack warned.

"But she does say that, Daddy," Emma told him, her face an expression of earnestness before turning back to Kelsey. "She knows 'cuz she has an older brother."

Kelsey had to bite the inside of her cheek to keep from laughing out loud, or screaming in terror.

What had she gotten herself into? Why hadn't she just written down the recipe and gotten the hell out of there?

Yeah, she knew why. When Emma had looked up at her with those big blue eyes, she was a goner. Plus, Jack had messed up chocolate chip cookies. He couldn't be trusted with a recipe.

Besides, she was making nice. Okay, helping the kid with her cookies was going a bit above and beyond. Never let it be said Kelsey Reagan did things halfway.

"I liked having an older brother," Kelsey said when she noticed Emma staring up at her. She'd *loved* having an older brother. Her entire life, no one mattered more to her than Dillon. He'd been her protector and best friend. And that awful night when she'd made the biggest mistake of her life, he'd even been her savior.

"Are you sad?"

She didn't know what surprised her more. Emma's question or the comforting feel of a small hand on her arm.

"No. I was just—"

"You look sad." Emma patted her arm and Kelsey thought her heart would simply burst in her chest. "Is your brother in heaven?"

"No," she said while Jack snorted, presumably at the idea of Dillon standing at the heavenly gates. "But you know what?" She removed the girl's hand from her arm. "Even though I liked having a big brother, your friend was right, too. Sometimes he was a real pain in the butt."

As she'd intended, Emma giggled and the tension in the room eased.

"It's way past your bedtime, Emma." Jack wiped his hands on a dish towel. "Time to hit the sack."

She stuck her lower lip out. "Do I have to?"

"Yes. You have to. What do you say to Kelsey?"

Like a well-trained child, she automatically responded, "Thank you."

"Don't worry about—"

The rest of Kelsey's words stuck in her throat when Emma threw her arms around her neck and squeezed tight.

Now what was she supposed to do? She looked to Jack for guidance but the expression on his face told her he wasn't any happier with the turn of events than she was.

Still, she couldn't let the kid dangle there forever. She awkwardly patted Emma's back, careful not to be too rough. Before she could decide holding the soft, cuddly body of a kid wasn't all that bad, Jack pulled Emma away.

"Go brush your teeth," he said, placing Emma on the floor. "I'll be up in a few minutes to tuck you in."

"Okay." Emma yawned and sent Kelsey a sleepy smile. "Good night."

"Night." Kelsey cleared her throat, kept her eyes on Emma's retreating figure. "Well, I guess I'll be—"

"Did you think I would lay off your brother just because you helped my daughter make cookies?"

She blinked. Not so much at Jack's question or the coolness of his voice, but at how her stomach fell in response to his anger. To his accusation.

"Excuse me?"

"Did you think I'd pull strings for Ward?" He walked over to her slowly and she couldn't fight the feeling she was being stalked. "What did you hope to achieve here?"

"Those." She inclined her head toward the cookies. "Mission accomplished."

"Out on the porch you said you were going to do me a favor. And favors usually come with strings attached. Is that what this is all about? You think I'll owe you now?"

Because his accusation hurt more than she would've liked—and way more than she ever would've admitted—she forced out a laugh. "I didn't do this for any reason other than to help the kid."

"You expect me to believe you helped Emma out of the goodness of your heart?"

The derision in his voice turned her hurt into anger. Anger that she seized with both hands and held on to for dear life.

"I don't lie." Not anymore.

It was the need to get back at him that made her edge forward until their thighs brushed. The heat in Jack's eyes became more intense. More exciting. And way more frightening.

Ignoring good sense, she slid both hands up his chest. His body tensed and a breath hissed out from between his teeth. With a small smile, she wrapped her arms around his neck and pressed her body against his.

"Besides, if I really wanted you to go easy on Dillon or look the other way or whatever it is you're accusing me of," she said in a husky voice as she rocked her hips against him suggestively, "I could think of something much more…interesting to offer you than cookies."

CHAPTER EIGHT

JACK KNEW SHE WAS MESSING with him but he couldn't stop himself from reacting to her nearness. Her scent. Her heat.

His hands trembled with the need to pull her closer, to slip under her shirt and caress her silky skin. He wanted to smooth his fingers up her bare legs and run his tongue over the delicate skin at her collar bone. To dip his head and taste the surprising sweetness of her kiss once again.

He stepped back until Kelsey's hands fell from around his neck. "I don't like being used."

Mostly, he didn't like the idea of her selling herself short. Not to him, or anyone else for that matter. Especially not to help her brother.

"If I were to *use* you," she said huskily, "I doubt you'd have any complaints."

He studied her. Her voice was assured, she wore a cocky grin, but something in her eyes made him suspicious.

"So you're here to screw me?" he asked evenly.

If he hadn't been studying her so closely, he might've missed her slight flinch, but there was no way he could've missed the color reddening her cheeks or the indignation in her expression. She opened her mouth, more than likely readying yet another lie.

"Why don't you cut the act?" he asked. "What are you really doing here?"

She picked at the bottom of her skirt. "It's not important."

"Let me be the judge of that."

She shrugged. "After our little…run-in this morning, I spoke with Dillon."

He waited. When she didn't go on, he prompted, "And?"

"And…" She blew out a breath. "And I sort of told him how we—" she gestured between them "—sort of had an argument and he was…well…he asked me to, you know, smooth things over with you." She rushed on, "But not because he's looking for special favors or anything."

"You came over to apologize?" he asked carefully. Out of all the scenarios he could've imagined, her wanting to apologize for giving him a hard time hadn't crossed his mind.

"Something like that," she muttered.

"That still doesn't explain the whole cookie thing with Emma."

She pressed her lips together. "I can relate to what she's going through. When my mother wasn't tending bar, she was either passed out or on her way to being passed out." Kelsey stuck her hands in her pockets, which pulled her skirt even lower and exposed more of her smooth, flat stomach. He forced himself to keep his eyes on her face. "I was always the one to go to school with dirty clothes and a lunch that consisted of peanut butter on stale bread."

She stood still, her chin raised, her eyes on his. He'd give her one thing, she had courage. She didn't hide. Even when she spoke about something that was obviously hard on her, she met it straight on.

"How is that like Emma?" he asked in his cop voice. Emotionless. Detached.

"When I was around her age, it was my turn to bring in a treat. The teacher took me aside, told me she could bring in something and tell the class it was from me." Kelsey frowned as if she was still angry at her teacher for trying to help her. "I told her I'd bring in something myself."

Jack could easily picture her as a little girl. All skinny arms and legs, a mop of red hair and a mile-long stubborn streak.

"After school that day," she continued, "I went home and bugged Dillon to help me. He took me to the library where we found a recipe that was user-friendly and cheap. We made the cookies and I took them to school the next day."

"Daddy," Emma called from the top of the stairs.

"I'll be up in a minute, honey."

He turned back to the sexy, surprising woman before him. Not that he'd changed his mind about keeping his distance from her, but it wouldn't hurt him to ease up on her a bit.

"Sounds like you and Ward had a rough childhood," he said, neutral.

"You don't know the half of it."

Jack frowned as he realized he wanted to know all of it.

"What about your father?" he finally asked.

Her pretty mouth thinned. "What about him?"

"Wasn't he in the picture?"

"He took off before I was born."

"So it was just you and Ward and your mother? That must've been tough."

"Not really. Besides, it was rarely just the three of us. More like the three of us and whatever man my mother was sleeping with at the time."

"What about Dillon?" he asked as he turned and opened the door to his refrigerator. He took out two cans of soda and pushed the door closed with his foot. "Was he in trouble a lot when he was younger?" He held out a can of soda to her.

She stared at the soda, the expression on her sexy face growing darker with each passing second. "What the hell is this?"

He glanced down. "It's cola. You don't want it? I have beer or—"

"I'm not talking about the soda," she hissed as she straightened and slapped her hands on her hips, "and you damn well know it."

Hell, yes, he knew it. But he wasn't ready to admit it quite yet. He schooled his features into a puzzled expression. "I'm not following you."

"Oh, you're not only following me, you're interrogating me."

Jack stepped forward. She straightened and lifted her chin. He ignored how she tensed when his hand brushed her arm as he set one of the cans down on the table. He eased back and opened his own soda, took a long drink.

When he lowered the can, she was still looking at him like he kicked puppies for entertainment. "This isn't an interrogation. It's a conversation."

"What you're doing is fishing for information." She sneered. "What's the matter? Aren't you man enough to come right out and ask what you want to know?"

He ground his back teeth together. She sure had a thing about challenging his manhood. "I'm…curious about you."

She snorted out a laugh. "Right. You want to know what makes me tick, huh? What's made me the woman I am today."

"I want to help you, Kelsey." He said it quietly, and realized he meant it. He did want to find out more about her. To figure her out. But only because she was such a damn puzzle, he assured himself.

One he fully intended to solve.

He met her eyes, willed her to believe him. To trust him. "Talk to me. Tell me why you're so willing to stick up for Ward. Why are you so loyal to the man who killed your step-father in cold blood?"

KELSEY'S THROAT CONSTRICTED and her mouth grew dry. She snatched the soda off the table, popped the top and took a deep gulp of the cold liquid. It didn't help ease the dryness much, but it gave her time to gather her thoughts.

She could feel Jack's eyes on her. Intense. Probing. As if he could break through her barriers and see all her secrets if only he looked hard enough. Waited long enough.

"What'd you do? Look into my brother's past or something?"

Jack stuck his free hand in his pocket. "I ran a background check on Ward when he first moved here."

"You run background checks on all your town's new citizens?" Not that she was worried about him looking into her past. Her records were sealed. She watched him thoughtfully. "Then again, someone like you probably does."

He narrowed his eyes. "What is that supposed to mean?"

"Someone all upstanding and righteous."

"You make it sound like there's something wrong with being upstanding. And I didn't check Ward's background for my own pleasure or to appease my curiosity. I did it because he was applying to rent from a friend of mine."

"Did this friend ask you to check up on my brother?"

"She didn't have to—"

"In other words, no."

He scowled. "Surprisingly, people with less than exemplary backgrounds don't always go around announcing that fact. Besides, that's what friends do. They look out for one another. They don't wait to be asked for help."

She wouldn't know. She didn't have any friends. "Who is this 'friend'?"

He hesitated. "Nina Carlson. She runs Sweet Suggestions for her grandparents."

She raised her eyebrows. "So she allowed Dillon to rent from her, anyway? I bet that just fries your bacon."

"I'm not thrilled that a convicted murderer is living above a single mother of two," he admitted. "Or that he's befriended my sister."

"Dillon would never hurt—"

"He killed a man."

"You don't know anything about what happened that night," she said, unable to keep her voice from shaking.

"Why don't you tell me?"

Oh, he was good. When he looked at her with those mesmerizing eyes of his, when he spoke to her in that gentle, cajoling tone, she wanted to trust him. To believe him.

God, but she was pathetic.

"Why should I tell you anything? You'll just twist whatever I say to suit your own needs."

His eyes flashed but his voice remained unaffected as he said, "I want to hear your side of things. You want to help your brother. That's understandable. Commendable. But loyalty only goes so far—"

"Not where I'm standing it doesn't."

"And the best thing you can do for Ward is to talk him into coming clean. If he did hit Shannon, if things got out of hand or out of his control, the jury will take that into consideration." His voice was calm, low and soothing. It made her want to tear her hair out. Or better yet, tear his hair out. Strand by short, dark strand.

"You really are a cop, aren't you?" She could overlook him thinking the worst of her, for believing she'd come over to sway him into going easy on Dillon.

What she couldn't overlook was him trying to get her to think, even briefly, that he could possibly be different. That maybe she could trust him.

A muscle jumped in his jaw. "I want to help you."

"You want to help yourself."

"I don't want to see you messed up in this. If your brother is dangerous—"

"Oh, for God's sake," she said, tossing her hands in the air. "I know my brother, okay? He didn't kill that woman and he isn't dangerous."

"He did time in prison," he said flatly, "for murder."

As if she needed reminding of that. "He was convicted of manslaughter. And there were extenuating circumstances."

"There always are," he said.

"Dillon didn't mean to kill Glenn—"

"Glenn? Was that your stepfather?"

She curled her fingers into her palms, her short nails digging into her flesh. "Glenn Hopkins was the jerk my mother married, yes."

Memories of that awful night assaulted her. Dragged her back through time. The sight of Glenn looming over her, his pale, fleshy face inches from her own. His brown eyes glassy and filled with so much hatred, so much violence that even though she knew he was long dead and buried, even though she was safe and he could never hurt her again, Kelsey shivered.

She rubbed her hands over her chilled arms and viciously pushed aside the memories. "The only reason Dillon fought with Glenn that night was to protect me."

His gaze sharpened. "I thought your brother pleaded guilty."

"Look, it doesn't matter—"

"Wait a minute," he said and held up a hand as if the gesture could stop time along with her words. "Let me get this straight. You say Ward killed your stepfather to protect you?"

"That's right."

"But that information was never introduced in court or during his plea agreement?"

She shrugged and, because she couldn't stand there a moment longer with Jack's disbelief boring into her head, got up from the table and crossed to the counter. The distance made it easier. "The public defender said it wouldn't change anything."

"Seems to me his attorney could've used it to go to trial."

"Yeah, well, he didn't think I would make a good witness."

"Why not?"

Dillon's cynical public defender had been part of the good-old boy's network in their small town. He'd told Kelsey she would be a hindrance to the case. That the prosecutor would rip her testimony and her already torn reputation to shreds.

He'd also made it clear he wouldn't be able to get a jury to believe her story when he didn't believe it himself.

"Does it matter? Dillon did plead guilty and, instead of the easy sentence his attorney promised, the judge threw the book at him."

"His sentence didn't seem unfair to me."

"How can you say that? You checked into Dillon's past. He wasn't violent. He didn't have any priors. He was straight as an arrow."

God, how her brother's Boy Scout tendencies used to drive her nuts. Now she'd give anything to see even the merest hint of the old Dillon.

"You think I don't know what's going on here?" she continued. "It's the same thing that happened to him before. He can't win."

"What are you talking about?"

"It hadn't helped matters that Glenn wasn't just an ordinary abusive stepfather and husband. He was also a cop. Or, at the time, an ex-cop. But he still had friends on the force. Still had people who would turn the other way while he kicked the crap out of my mother and Dillon."

Oh, the local cops would come to the house—hard not to when the neighbors complained of the noise and fighting. But all the cops did was pull Glenn off of whichever one of them he was pummeling and take him somewhere to sober up.

Jack crushed his soda can and threw it into the recycling bin with more force than necessary. "He ever hit you?"

"Only if I was slow enough to let him catch me—which wasn't often. Besides, Dillon looked out for me."

He'd looked out for her and she'd let him down. And in the process cost him his freedom, and his future.

She lifted her head and her eyes locked with Jack's. She read his compassion, curiosity and something…deeper.

His compassion got her back up. The curiosity she could evade. But her body responded to the something deeper. She wanted to cross the tiny room, slide into his arms and just…be held. Comforted. She wanted to ease the constant ache in her heart, if only for a minute or two.

What she wanted was standing before her, strong and competent and honorable. What she wanted was Jack.

Man, she was in such deep trouble here.

He scrubbed a hand over his jaw. "I understand why you think your brother got the shaft, but—"

"Forget it," she said hollowly. "It's obvious you don't believe me."

"I didn't say that."

"You didn't have to. I can see it on your face."

"Damn it, Kelsey, I—"

"Daddy…" Emma whined loudly from upstairs. "Where are you?"

"You'd better go," Kelsey said, glad for the interruption.

"I'm coming, Emma," he called and then pinned Kelsey to the spot with his intense gaze. "I won't be long and when I'm done, we can finish this discussion."

He didn't move. She didn't know what he was waiting for, so she nodded. Then, as soon as she heard him climbing the stairs, she grabbed her purse and ran like hell.

JACK MANAGED TO GET THROUGH the nightly ritual of tucking Emma into bed—complete with prayers and kisses—in record time. It seemed like mere moments after leaving Kelsey in his kitchen, he was racing back down the stairs.

Jack shook his head as he descended. Emma had included Kelsey in her prayers. He hoped Emma wasn't getting her hopes up that there was even the slightest chance of Kelsey being a part of their lives.

Kelsey was still holding back from him. But he planned on getting the truth out of her tonight. He whipped the apron over his head, crumpled it into a ball and tossed it in a corner. After running a hand over his hair and taking a deep breath, he walked into the kitchen.

The empty kitchen.

He thumped his fist repeatedly against his thigh. Damn it. He should've handcuffed her to the refrigerator.

He pulled a beer out of the fridge, twisted off the top and sat down heavily at the kitchen table. Reaching behind him, he grabbed two cookies off the counter. The taste of chocolate melted on his tongue and he leaned back and grabbed two more.

He shouldn't be surprised she'd taken off. She obviously didn't want him asking too many more questions about the night Ward killed her stepfather.

But why? he wondered, wiping a hand on his jeans and washing away the sweetness of the cookies with a swallow of beer. Because she was telling the truth and it was still too painful to talk about? Or because she was lying?

If she was telling the truth, it sure as hell explained her blatant animosity toward cops. Compassion stirred in him for the child Kelsey had been, for what she'd gone through. And he could only imagine what her stepfather had tried to do to her. What had pushed her brother to kill another man in order to save her.

Jack wasn't stupid. He knew there were officers out there who abused their power, and that the code of silence protected them. Wearing a badge didn't automatically make someone honorable or trustworthy.

He drank another swallow of beer and leaned back, balancing his weight on the chair's rear legs. Did it even make a difference? So far, the evidence pointed to her brother being guilty of another murder. Whether or not Ward killed his stepfather to protect Kelsey shouldn't figure into the here and now.

And it didn't, but it also didn't stop Jack from wanting to know what really happened that night. From wanting Kelsey to tell him what happened.

He rotated his head from side to side, rolled his shoulders back. He doubted that would ever happen. Kelsey obviously wasn't going to volunteer the information and he wasn't going to spend any more time trying to pry it out of her. He wasn't going to spend any more time with her at all unless it was in a professional capacity.

So what if he wanted her? It was just lust. He absently rubbed a hand over his stomach. He could fight his body's reaction to her.

The coroner's report should be ready tomorrow, Tuesday at the latest. And while he wouldn't have the DNA reports for at least a month, he hoped he'd have enough evidence to make an arrest within the next two weeks.

An arrest that would put a murderer behind bars and send Kelsey back to New York where she belonged.

CHAPTER NINE

A COLD, DRIZZLING RAIN came down as Jack made his way to The Summit's door the next day. He stepped inside and ran a hand through his damp hair. He spotted Allie in the back corner scrubbing a table as if soap and elbow grease could wash away forty-odd years of grime and smoke residue.

"It's bad enough you befriended Ward—the only convicted felon in the tricounty area," he said as he headed toward her. "Now you're letting his sister stay upstairs?"

"Hello to you, too," she said.

"Hello." He stopped next to her. "Now, about Kelsey—"

"My relationship with Dillon is none of your concern, and Kelsey got kicked out of The Bee Hive. Was I supposed to let her sleep on the street?"

Jack pressed his fingers against his gritty eyes. "It used to be cute when you brought home all those unwanted cats and dogs," he said on a long sigh. "And the time you found that bullfrog and insisted he needed to see the vet because he sounded hoarse was a riot. But aren't you too old to collect strays?"

She straightened and sent him an arch look. "A word of advice. If you want to live a long, healthy, relatively pain-free life, don't ever tell a woman she's too old."

He rolled his eyes. "I'll make a note of that."

"Good." She picked the bucket up off the floor. Dirty water sloshed over the side and onto Jack's already wet shoe. "Kelsey will only be here until this misunderstanding with Dillon is straightened out."

He shook the beaded water off his foot. "You know this is more than just a misunderstanding."

She skirted around him and began scrubbing the next table. "Any new developments?"

"Are you asking as my sister? Or as Ward's attorney?"

"I'm asking as your sister and Dillon's friend."

"In that case, no. Nothing new."

The coroner's report he'd received that morning had simply reiterated what Jack had already guessed. Estimated time of death; between 11:30 p.m. and 2:00 a.m. Cause of death: massive brain hemorrhage caused by two blows to the head with a blunt object. The second, a stronger blow, had killed her. And while it was discovered that Shannon had engaged in sexual activity that night, nothing indicated it was anything but consensual.

Allie stomped to another table, her bucket swinging wildly in her hand. Seemed he'd made her mad. No surprise. He'd spent the entire day making people angry, starting with the men and women in his department when he'd attempted to get to the bottom of who'd leaked the story to Dora Wilkins over the weekend.

Naturally, no one had stepped forward and taken the blame.

Then the overworked technician at the state lab had bitten Jack's head off when he'd called to see if there was any possible way to put a rush on his evidence—especially the mud samples. Add two irate phone calls from city council members, and he was having one hell of a day.

"Coroner's finished with the autopsy," he said, extending an olive branch to Allie. "Shannon's body has been released to Mark. The funeral will be on Wednesday."

"Good."

"Back to Ward's sister—"

"Save it, Jack." Allie moved on to the next table. "She's here and she's staying. Besides, I like her. She's been a godsend around here, and now that Tina's quit—"

"When did that happen?"

"This morning. She's moving back to Buffalo. She and her ex-husband are going to try and work things out. So Kelsey's going to cover her shift for the time being."

That calm and reasonable lawyer-tone she used made his back teeth ache. "Now she's got you hiring her?"

"She didn't *get* me to hire her. I needed a bartender and she's filling in. What's the big deal?"

"Other than the fact that her brother is a murder suspect?"

"You still here?"

Jack turned to find Kelsey walking toward them from the kitchen.

She strode past him with no more than a cursory glance, her attention on Allie. "I thought you had an appointment at three."

Allie ran the back of her hand over her forehead. "I do. Why? What time is it?"

"Quarter till."

Allie cursed and dropped her cleaning rag on the table. "I have to go." She raced out of the room and into the kitchen. When she came back, she was slipping on a tan blazer and had a large, brown purse in her hand. "I'll be back in about an hour." She took the time to pin Jack with a threatening look. "Behave."

The door shut behind Allie, and Jack shoved his hands in his pockets. He wasn't in the mood to get into yet another argument. Although, to be honest, Kelsey didn't seem too inclined to argue with him. Hell, she didn't seem too inclined to even talk to him. She'd barely looked his way since coming into the room and was now studiously ignoring him.

Which suited him just fine. He had better things to do than stand there and watch her pretend he didn't exist. He turned to leave when she began pushing one of the tables across the floor.

The sight of her bent over, her round ass sticking up... He even took a step forward, his hand out to touch her, before catching himself. He fisted his fingers but couldn't tear his gaze away. Which she must've sensed because she stopped and swung her head around.

And dear, sweet God, the sight of her looking back at him over her shoulder turned him rock hard.

"Enjoying the view?"

A denial sprang to his lips but he bit it back. He might be perverted but he wasn't a liar.

"Yes, actually," he said as he held her gaze. "I am enjoying looking at you. Very much."

KELSEY REARED UP and faced Jack. Gooseflesh rose on her arms. He walked toward her, his inscrutable eyes locked on hers. Abruptly she turned back to the table.

"Allie will probably be gone awhile," she blurted out in an attempt to change the subject. The subject she had idiotically brought up. "You might not want to wait."

"Where did she take off to?"

Was that humor in his voice? Could he tell she was flustered? Damn it, she never got flustered.

Not until she'd met Jack.

"She, uh, had a meeting with the head of advertising at the radio station. She wants to record an ad for the bar."

He came up behind her. She *felt* him, felt his body heat, smelled his musky scent. "Was that your idea?"

She swallowed. "Advertising the bar? No. That's all your sister's doing."

Desperate to put some much needed distance between them, she bent her head and resumed pushing the table.

"Let me help with that." He strode to the other side, stopping her from going any farther. "Where do you want it?" He lifted his end with an ease that got on her nerves.

"I can handle this. I only have a few more to go."

He glanced at the four tables behind her. "You still have all the chairs to put back. If I pitch in, you'll get done that much faster."

She huffed out a breath. "Aren't you working?"

"I'm always working."

Wasn't that the truth? And something she'd be wise to remember.

Today, the fact he was all cop was brought home by the sight of him in his uniform for the first time. Black cargo-style pants, a drab-green button up shirt and a shiny badge pinned to his chest.

She'd never before been turned on by a man in uniform. There was a first time for everything.

"I'm sure you have better things to do than rearrange tables."

"Not at the moment. And I'm officially off-duty in ten minutes." He scratched his jaw. Her own fingers itched to touch the hard planes of his face, feel the roughness of his shadowed beard. "If you want, you could consider it payback for the cookies. Since I never thanked you in person."

"Yeah, well, I couldn't stick around all night," she mumbled, warmth spreading across her neck and face.

She wasn't sure which was more humiliating. The fact that she'd run from him last night, or the fact that he knew it.

She shrugged. "We're going to start by the pool table—" she jerked her head toward it "—and work our way out diagonally."

Jack walked backward. "Quiet here today. Isn't Ward working?"

Though she tried to fight it, she couldn't help but be disappointed. "Is this going to be one of your not-so-subtle attempts to interrogate me about my brother? Because if it is—"

"It was a simple question."

"None of your questions are simple." They set the table down. "If you're doing this—" she gestured to the table "—as some sort of ploy—"

"It's no ploy."

"Well, then, why don't we agree to keep any mention of Dillon or Shannon Crandall out of the conversation? Better yet, let's not talk at all."

He nodded shortly and they walked back to the remaining tables in silence. It wasn't until they'd set the final table down and were heading back for the chairs that Jack spoke again.

"Allie told me you're helping her out around here. Giving her advice. You work in the bar-restaurant business?"

"I thought we weren't conversing?"

"That was only one option."

"That was the option I voted for." Otherwise, it was too easy to allow him to lull her into a false sense of complacency. Damn it, whenever they spoke it was too easy to like him.

When he merely raised an eyebrow she grudgingly admitted, "I tend bar."

He lifted a stack of chairs and Kelsey's mind went blank. God, he was gorgeous. His biceps strained against his short sleeves, the muscles in his back bunched and flexed under his shirt. She caught her breath. Oh, my.

Off-limits, she reminded herself as her gaze followed his progress across the room. Totally, one hundred percent, hands off, shouldn't be staring at his ass or wanting to touch him off-limits.

He set the chairs down, lifted his head and caught her eye. One side of his mouth quirked as if he'd effectively read her mind. "Where do you work?"

She hastily picked up two chairs. "Place in Tribeca called The Rat Pack."

"I've never heard of it."

"You're not missing much. It's one of those new dance clubs where the decor's trendy, the music's loud and the customers all think they're living a real-life version of *Sex and the City*."

"Sounds like you really enjoy your job."

She ignored his dry tone. Concentrated on carrying two more chairs across the room. "It paid the rent, and I'm good at it. Or was good at it. I don't, technically, work at The Rat Pack anymore."

"Why not?"

His question seemed innocent. But she couldn't shake the feeling it went far beyond mere curiosity.

"Things at work have been…tense for a while now."

Yeah. Tense. Well, that's what happened when you made the colossal mistake of sleeping with your boss just because you were at a low point in your life and he happened to resemble George Clooney.

If it was dark. And you squinted your eyes.

"Kelsey, did you lose your job because of Ward?"

"What? No." She laughed humorlessly. "My boss gave me a hard time about taking time off, but he didn't fire me. I quit."

Finished with the chairs, he leaned back against a table and crossed his arms. "Because of your brother."

"No. I would've quit, anyway."

He studied her silently. An old cop trick for getting people to open up. As someone who'd spent a lot of time being questioned by cops, she knew all their tricks.

Unfortunately, it worked. At least on her.

She found herself saying, "I made a mistake. My boss, Eric…well…to make a long story short, a few months ago—due to some very poor judgment and a bit too much alcohol—I slept with him. Unfortunately, since Eric managed to get me into bed once, his new mission in life is a repeat performance. When I made it clear it wasn't going to happen again, he started complaining about my work and giving me the worst shifts…" She chanced a glance at him. "You can see where this is going, right?"

"If your boss is harassing you," he said neutrally, "you can bring him up on charges."

"Why? It was my own fault. I figure I got what I deserved." She picked up the rag and bucket Allie had left and carried them behind the bar. "Though, to tell the truth, just having sex with him would've been punishment enough."

She felt, more than saw, him glance at her. Thought she heard the sound of his choked laughter.

But when she looked at him, his face was expressionless. "Why did you sleep with him? You don't seem like the type of woman to let a few drinks make her decisions for her."

That much was true, and his insight made her feel warm inside. "It...uh...was a combination of factors really. The alcohol just made it easier to make the wrong decision."

And she'd already admitted way more than she'd ever wanted to. She hadn't told anyone about that night—it wasn't exactly high on her short list of accomplishments. Yet there she was, blabbing to Jack for all she was worth.

He was tricky and he was smart. She had to get rid of him before she told him all her secrets. "Well, thanks for your help. I guess you'll be go—"

"Does Allie have any bottled water around here?"

She blinked. "Uh...yeah...in the kitchen. I'll get you one."

It's okay, she reassured herself as she pushed through the swinging doors. She nabbed a bottle of water from the fridge and kicked the door shut. Closing her eyes, she took a deep breath. Everything would be okay. She'd give Jack his water and he'd leave. That's what she needed to gain her equilibrium. She couldn't think when he was around. He made her edgy. Nervous.

Damn, she hated being nervous.

She opened her eyes, turned and gasped in surprise to find herself trapped. Trapped by the table at her back, and Jack's lean, hard body in front of her.

"Here's your water," she said and shoved it into his stomach.

Except her shove didn't back him up. Instead, he smiled as he accepted the bottle and twisted the cap off. "Thanks."

She kept her eyes straight ahead, stared at his throat as he drank. An enticing patch of skin was visible at his unbuttoned collar. Her pulse kicked into overdrive.

He lowered the now empty bottle. Tossed it into the trash can in the corner. "What factors?"

She jerked her gaze up. "Huh? What?"

"What factors induced you to sleep with your boss?"

See? Tricky. She pushed ineffectively at his chest. "Back off. I can't think when you crowd me."

"Really?" Though his expression remained neutral, humor lit his eyes. "That's interesting."

She didn't think it was interesting at all. Annoying? A little bit. Frightening? Possibly.

Exciting? Definitely.

He didn't move. Just stood there staring down at her. Pressure continued to build in her chest, not easing until he finally stepped back.

"Everything all right?" he asked when she remained rooted to her spot.

She let out a shaky breath. "Fine."

Why wouldn't it be all right? She had no job, had spent her last dime trying to find her brother—who wanted nothing to do with her and was the prime suspect in a murder investigation. And last, but not least, she had the hots for the cop who wanted to toss her brother back in prison. A man with a daughter and that whole white picket fence deal she'd figured out long ago she wasn't meant for. A man she didn't trust, who didn't trust her.

Oh, yeah. Everything was just dandy.

KELSEY STILL HADN'T MOVED, and Jack sure as hell wasn't backing up any farther. Not when her scent filled his head and his body was reacting.

"Are you going to ignore my question all afternoon?"

"It doesn't matter."

"It might." It mattered to him. "If you're embarrassed—"

"I'm *not* embarrassed," she replied indignantly.

He'd obviously hit a nerve. "Good. Because I'm not judging you."

Her disbelief was plain. "Aren't you?"

He kept quiet. Just looked at her. Which was no hardship. As he'd told her earlier, he liked looking at her. Her sharp features, her slender body. The way her teeth worried her plump lower lip when she was thinking.

"It was stupid," she finally said. "I was stupid."

"I'm discovering you are many things. But stupid isn't one of them."

She blushed. "Yeah, well, the day I…the reason I…messed up…was because I'd just found out Leigh, my mother, had died. It threw me, and I let my guard down. Eric was there and I…I guess I needed someone."

"Grief can play havoc on a person." He knew that better than anyone.

She tipped her head to the side exposing her long, pale neck. He rubbed itching palms down the legs of his jeans.

"Did it you?" she asked.

"Did what me?"

"Did grief mess you up when your wife died?"

"For a while," he said slowly, his stomach tightening as he remembered those first few months after Nicole's death.

How much he'd hurt, how alone he'd been. "I had a rough period, but I managed to get through it."

"I can't imagine you allowing anything, not even grief to control you."

"I'm not infallible, Kelsey," he said quietly. God knew that was the truth. But maybe if he opened up to her, she'd respond in kind. He forced himself to meet her eyes, to face the possible derision, the disappointment he'd see there once she knew what he'd done. "Because of my grief, I made a bad decision. I wasn't thinking straight and went against my supervisor's orders. I almost lost my badge because I mishandled a case I was working. Worse than that, because of me and those actions, an innocent man died."

CHAPTER TEN

SURPRISE AND SYMPATHY softened Kelsey's features. "What happened?"

"Nicole, my wife, was a high-school English teacher. She was dedicated to her students. She wanted to make a difference in their lives. For the most part, she succeeded."

He hesitated, the only sound in the room the hum of the refrigerator. Not many people knew the truth, how far he'd sunk after Nicole's death. How he'd gone against everything he'd believed in and risked his badge and reputation in an effort to follow in her footsteps.

"A few months after she died," he continued, "I picked up one of her students for armed robbery. He'd been in trouble before and Nicole had tried to help him. She'd believed, had hoped, he could change."

Kelsey raised an eyebrow. "You didn't."

"She was an optimist. I'm a realist. But when I brought that kid in, even though my gut told me he was guilty, I kept thinking about Nicole and what she'd want me to do."

"Which was?"

"To help him out. To give him a second chance." His hands were clenched and he deliberately straightened his fingers. "We had surveillance video from the store showing it was the kid's partner, and not him, who'd held the gun. So, we let him cut a deal. Instead of going to jail, he was back on the streets. Ten days later, while robbing another convenience store, he shot and killed the clerk."

"Is that why you came back to Serenity Springs?"

He shoved his hands in his pockets. "Part of the reason. I ended up being reprimanded for allowing that kid to cut a deal against my lieutenant's approval. It was then that I realized the only reason I did it was for…"

"For your wife?"

He nodded. "So you see? Grief affects people in different ways. It's understandable if you—"

"You don't get it. What you did was out of love for your wife. I didn't sleep with Eric because I was looking for comfort or because I was grief-stricken. There was nothing. No loss. No pain or sadness. My mother was dead, and I felt nothing."

Jack wasn't so sure about that. Seemed she'd been hurting in her own way. "Either way, you made a mistake. We all do."

"It's not the same," she insisted as if she couldn't allow it to be the same. "Okay, so you were hurting and made a judgment call that came back to bite you in the ass. I bet that doesn't happen often. I bet most of the time you think through each and every action before making a move. Gather your thoughts before saying a word. You're everything I'm not. Reserved. Cautious. Controlled."

Her words whipped through him like a brisk, autumn wind and he felt the thin thread of his control snap.

"How reserved would you think I was if I admitted I wanted you in my bed?" He closed the remaining distance between them, edging forward until their thighs met and her warmth seeped through his clothes. "How cautious if I said I find you completely sexy and exciting as hell? How controlled if I admitted thoughts of being with you have been driving me crazy since the moment I first saw you?" He had to touch her, so he ran a finger down her cheek before gently cupping the back of her neck.

Her eyes widened. "There are reasons we shouldn't—"

"I want you, and I'm not sure how much longer I can pretend I don't."

The pulse at the base of Kelsey's throat beat wildly, matching the erratic beat of his own heart. And then, because he couldn't *not* do it, he pressed his nose to the side of her neck and breathed her in.

Her body twitched and she laid her hands on his chest, but she didn't push him away. A fact he was extremely grateful for as he inhaled deeply again and brushed his lips across her skin.

She gasped. Jack took that as a good sign. Anything that didn't involve her stopping him was a good sign. He slid his free hand around her waist and pulled her to him.

He pressed kisses the length of her neck. Flicked his tongue out to taste her skin. When he bit down gently on her rapid pulse, her fingers dug into his skin. Her deep moan seemed to reach into his pants and wrap around his groin like warm, teasing fingers.

"Oh, man," she said huskily. "I don't think—"

He set his lips against hers to silence her. He didn't want her to think. Didn't want either of them to think. If it meant not kissing her, not touching her, he might never think again.

When her hands slowly slid up his chest, when her lips softened and her mouth finally opened under his, his sense of relief made him dizzy. Or maybe it was her tongue against his, the sweet taste of her that made his knees weak and his heart heavy.

She felt so incredibly good. He continued his assault on her mouth, he used his lips, his tongue, his teeth until they were both breathing hard, both frantic in their need to get closer.

Still kissing her, Jack set both hands on her waist and lifted her onto the table. Easing himself between her thighs did little to alleviate the ache in his groin. He placed his hands behind her knees, spread her legs and wrapped them around his own waist. The contact hit him like a bolt of lightning.

Nestled intimately the way he was, he couldn't stop himself from rubbing against her softness and heat. She groaned, low and deep into his mouth and raised her hips in a silent plea.

Half-mad with wanting her, he continued to kiss her deeply as he laid her back on the table. He wanted to climb up and settle his weight on her more than he wanted his next breath.

Her legs slid down the outside of his thighs to dangle limply over the table edge.

He kissed his way down her throat. Easing his hands under the hem of her shirt, he pushed the material up exposing her smooth, flat stomach and the top of her red tattoo and the silver belly-button stud—both of which he promised himself he'd return to later.

He pushed the shirt up. Caught his breath. She wore one of those fancy bras, a white one edged in lace, that pushed her breasts together and up so they almost spilled out of the silky material.

Jack smoothed a finger across the lace. "Pretty."

"I'm flat-chested."

He looked up to see a hint of vulnerability in her eyes. He shook his head and smiled at her. "Not flat. Small." Flicking the tiny clasp, he opened the bra. The air suddenly left his lungs. "You're beautiful."

He bent his head, suckled one hard, pink tip into his mouth, grunting in appreciation.

While he tongued her nipple, he rubbed her other breast, tweaked and pinched the nipple until she was writhing beneath him. He couldn't remember a time he'd wanted a woman more. Not even Nicole. He shoved the traitorous thought aside.

The incredibly sexy, breathy sounds she made played in his mind like a smoky jazz tune. She arched against his touch. Clawed at his shirt until it pulled free from his pants, and slid her soft, cool hands across his lower back, up his spine and down again.

He kissed his way to her other breast, lapped it into his mouth and sucked hard. Her body lifted underneath his touch and a cry escaped her.

He shifted lower, rubbing her nipples between his fingers as he trailed his mouth down her torso. He traced his finger-tip over the swirly edge of her tattoo and twirled his tongue around her belly button before pressing his mouth against the juncture of her thighs. She lifted her hips. Even through the thick material of her jeans he could smell her desire, knew she was wet and swollen for him.

A groan ripped from his throat. "You feel so good. This feels so good." He slid back up her body and kissed her again. "Let's go upstairs so we can—"

He broke off when Kelsey's head reared up and she frantically pushed at his shoulders while her legs kicked in her effort to get away. He straightened. Afraid that in her haste she was going to fall off the table, he attempted to help her up only to have her swat at him like he was a bug.

Jaw tight, he watched her roll to the side and slide off the table. She turned her back to him, adjusted her bra and pulled her shirt down to cover all that tempting skin he hadn't had enough of.

Aroused, and more than a little frustrated, Jack tipped his head back and heaved a breath. Damn it all to hell.

SHE WAS SHAKING. God, she was literally shaking. Kelsey closed her eyes and took an unsteady breath. What had she been thinking?

Well, she hadn't been thinking, that much was plain.

Her skin was sensitized to the point of aching, her clothes felt too tight, too constrictive, and her heart was beating hard enough to burst out of her chest.

"Kelsey?" Jack's voice washed over her causing her to shiver.

"What?" Longing and regret made her voice sharper than she intended.

She heard him sigh. "Could you look at me? Please?" he added quietly.

She pressed her lips together and finished adjusting her shirt. He stared at her intently as he tucked his own shirt back into his pants.

Kelsey laid a hand over her jittery stomach. She'd done that, had yanked at the stiff cloth, tugged at it in an attempt to get to the warm, smooth skin and taut muscles underneath.

"I apologize if I crossed a line," he said, his eyes steady on hers.

She frowned. Remembered how he'd immediately stopped when she'd made it clear she didn't want to go any further.

"You didn't." She cleared her throat. "Look, I'm...sorry if it seemed... I didn't mean to, you know, lead you on. I just..." Hadn't wanted to stop. And that realization had scared her to death.

"You have the right to stop. And you didn't lead me on. I kissed you, remember?"

Remember? She wasn't likely to forget. Ever.

She crossed her arms. "Well, I just wanted you to know that wasn't my intention. The leading on part."

He stepped toward her and she had to force herself not to back up. "If it wasn't for your brother, or my position as police chief, would we still be having this conversation?"

Or would we be having mind-blowing, earthshaking sex?

He didn't speak the words out loud, but she heard them as plainly as if he had. "I don't think it matters—"

"Probably not, but I'd like to know, anyway." When she remained silent, he smiled. "Humor me."

"If you'd asked me that a few days ago, I would've said no."

"What changed?"

"Well, even if you didn't want to lock up my brother—"

"I want to find whoever killed Shannon," he interrupted. "Whoever that may be."

"We still couldn't...get together."

"Because?"

Because he made her want too much. Things she couldn't have. Made her want to believe in him.

Since she couldn't tell him the truth, she said the first thing that popped into her head. "Because you have a kid."

"What does Emma have to do with us?"

"Nothing." Everything. "I just thought most single fathers were looking for a woman to take care of their kids for them. And I'm not looking to be anybody's wife. Or mother."

He looked like he'd been hit in the gut with a sledgehammer. "Mind telling me where that came from?"

It came from her being unable to risk having anyone depend on her. She knew she'd only let them down. "I don't know. That's the problem. How do I know you didn't kiss me as some sort of thank-you for helping Emma? Don't get the wrong idea about those cookies—"

He tipped his head back and roared with laughter, cutting her off. So glad to realize she amused him. Okay, so she did like hearing the sound of his deep laugh. Even if it was at her expense.

"I appreciate you helping us out," he said when he managed to control himself, "but those cookies didn't have anything to do with this."

"No?"

"I'm not looking for a mother for Emma. I kissed you because…" He shook his head. When he spoke again his voice was lower, deeper. More intimate. "I seem to have an awful hunger for you, Kelsey. One that, no matter how hard I fight it, isn't going away." He reached out and touched the ends of her hair before dropping his hand to his side. "I can't get you out of my head."

He cleared his throat. "Correct me if I'm wrong," he said into the silence, "but I thought you were attracted to me as well."

"You might find this hard to believe—" especially after she'd admitted what happened between her and Eric "—but I don't usually roll around on tables with a guy I'm not attracted to."

His lips twitched. "That's good to know. So, to clarify here, we're both single, unattached adults who are attracted to each other."

"Single, unattached adults who are on opposite sides of just about every issue I can think of. We're still right where we started. I can't turn my back on my brother. I won't."

And she couldn't get too close to Jack and Emma. Not if she wanted to keep her heart safe.

"And I won't do anything that jeopardizes this case. Or the integrity of the Serenity Springs Police Department."

"We're in agreement then." So why did she feel like crying? "Any involvement between us would only create problems. And I don't know about you, but I have enough crap to deal with."

"Do I even want to know what's going on here?"

Kelsey jerked around to see Dillon standing in the doorway. "Dillon, we were just… Jack wanted—"

"I think I have a pretty good idea about what Jack wants," her brother said, his anger palpable.

"We finished putting the tables and chairs back in the bar," Jack said. "Kelsey was kind enough to offer me a drink."

Dillon's mouth was tight as he looked at her, his eyes filled with suspicion. "As long as that's all she offered you."

Kelsey flinched, but before she could recover from her brother's verbal slap, Jack crossed the room. "Watch your step," he warned Dillon softly, "and watch your mouth."

Dillon didn't so much as blink. He sure didn't look intimidated. Of course, neither did Jack. And she'd thought it was tense in the room before? Ha.

"You can cut out the whole manly, testosterone-filled, silent-communication thing," Kelsey said. "It's pissing me off."

Worse, seeing her enigmatic brother and the contained cop go head-to-head was making her very, *very* nervous.

Finally, thankfully, Dillon stepped to the side and held his arm out in a gesture for Jack to pass by. "Will you be all right, Kelsey?" Jack asked.

She blinked. She knew what he meant. Would she be all right with Dillon? Would she be safe?

"I'll be fine."

"Are you sure?"

"She just said so, didn't she?" Dillon snapped.

Stony-faced, Jack waited. Her throat was too tight to speak, so she nodded.

Clearly frustrated, he didn't try to change her mind. He just walked away.

"What are you doing?" Dillon asked flatly when they were alone. "You must have gone insane if you're sleeping with the police chief."

She twisted her fingers together. "I'm not sleeping with Jack—with Chief Martin." But she couldn't deny she wanted to.

"Damn it, Kelsey, Jack Martin isn't someone you can play with."

"This isn't a game. And there's nothing going on between us."

"I hope not. How do you know he's not using you to get to me?"

"He's not," she said firmly. "He wouldn't."

She'd tasted the desire in his kiss. Felt it in the way he held her, touched her. He couldn't be pretending. Could he?

Dillon stabbed a hand through his hair. "I just…I want you to be careful."

"Why? You don't want anything to do with me, remember? Why do you care if I get hurt?"

He opened his mouth as if to deny it but then seemed to change his mind. "You're right," he said, and her stomach dropped. "I don't have to take care of you anymore. Besides, you never listened to me, anyway."

Kelsey slid bonelessly into a chair as Dillon stormed out of the room. She dropped her head to her hands. Oh, God. Dillon was right.

Growing up, she'd fought him and rebelled at every turn. Because of her, because she'd been unbelievably stubborn and immature and stupid, he'd had to rescue her from Glenn that night.

Now she was supposed to be helping her brother, not rolling around on the table with the man who wanted to send him to prison.

She groaned. Would she ever learn? Maybe her bastard of a stepfather had been right.

Maybe she really was nothing but trouble.

JACK TURNED UP THE COLLAR on his jacket and hunched his shoulders against the cold, pelting rain. He was surprised by the number of mourners standing by Shannon Crandall's freshly dug grave, their heads bowed slightly in prayer even as they fought the brisk wind for control of their umbrellas.

Seemed being the wife of one of Serenity Springs's more

prominent citizens guaranteed a well-attended funeral. Though Jack doubted any of the mourners—which, from his viewpoint looked to be most of the town's city officials and community leaders—would've given Shannon the time of day, dead or alive, if she hadn't been Mrs. Mark Crandall.

Jack stood by his Jeep, close enough to hear the priest's prayers, and far enough away to make it clear he wasn't there simply to pay his respects. He scanned the small crowd of mourners looking for the woman he'd come there to speak with. As his gaze drifted from one person to the next, he noticed the devastation on Mark Crandall's face. Most of the other mourners looked wet and cold and slightly bored, as if burying a young woman who'd been violently murdered was just another chore, an inconvenience they needed to get through before continuing on with their day.

His attention landed on a trim blonde standing next to Mayor Michaels. Though he couldn't see her features clearly, he knew she was the woman he was looking for. He straightened as the service ended. The blond woman walked alone, her head down, her large, black umbrella doing little to keep the rain off the front of her navy pantsuit. She stopped next to a brown rental car and opened the driver's side door.

Jack approached her. "Ms. Rennard? Tess Rennard?"

She looked up, her eyes rimmed red. "Yes?"

Tess Rennard's eyes were more gray than blue and her hair was two shades darker, but this close, Jack could easily see the similarities between Shannon and her older sister.

"Ms. Rennard, I'm Police Chief Jack Martin. We spoke on the phone a few days ago."

"Right." She fidgeted with the strap of her purse. Glanced around nervously. "Thanks for meeting me."

"Would you like to go somewhere more private?" he asked.

"I can't. I'm flying back to Florida—my plane leaves at three. That's why I asked you to meet me here."

"Okay." Jack waited until most of the mourners had hurried to the dryness and relative warmth of their vehicles before saying gently, "You said you had some information for me? About your sister?"

"Yeah." Tess dug into her purse and pulled out a pack of cigarettes and a pink disposable lighter. She tossed the purse into the car. "You told me to contact you if I remembered anything. Anything that might help you find who hurt Shannon."

When Jack had called Tess the day after Shannon's body had been discovered, she'd been too disturbed over her sister's death to give him much of anything. Except an earful for his—very delicate—suggestion that Shannon might have been unfaithful to her husband.

"That's right." Since it was raining too hard for him to take notes, he left his notebook in his inside jacket pocket. "Did you?"

"I don't know. Maybe." She tucked the handle of her umbrella between her shoulder and chin so she could light a cigarette. She blew out smoke on a long exhale. "She called me a few weeks ago. September 25. It was my birthday."

"Was that the last time you spoke to her?"

She nodded. "When we talked—you and me—I wasn't myself."

"You were distraught. It's understandable."

"I was," she readily agreed before taking another long drag of her cigarette. "And I was upset you were asking me such…personal questions about her. But afterwards…once I had a chance to calm down and think about it I…"

The wind picked up, the rain pelted his face, prickling his skin, but he kept his voice calm. Unhurried. "Ms. Rennard, I'm not passing judgment on Shannon or on how she lived her life. I'm trying to help."

She flicked the ash off her cigarette. "I guess I was trying to protect her. Protect her reputation." She cleared her throat. "But the truth is, Shannon did cheat on Mark. Often."

"Did she mention if Mr. Crandall became aware of her extramarital affairs?"

Her eyebrows drew together. "Not that I'm aware of."

"Did she mention anyone by name? Give any indication that her husband or someone else was threatening her?"

"Not threats, no. But she admitted she'd gotten herself into a situation."

"What kind of situation?"

"The last man she was…seeing—the last man she told me about—was quite a bit younger than her. She said at first she thought it was great. The attention. The way he was so easy to please and, more importantly, eager to please her."

"She never mentioned him by name?"

She tossed the cigarette on the ground. "All she said was that he was getting clingy, so she dumped him. He wanted her to leave Mark, which she never would've done."

"What about Mr. Crandall? If he learned of your sister's infidelities, would he ask her for a divorce?"

"No way. He worshipped her. I can't even say for sure he didn't know about her cheating on him. It wouldn't surprise me if he just chose to ignore it." She looked at her watch. "I'm sorry, but I have to get to the airport."

Jack stepped back. "I'll be in touch if I have any more questions. I appreciate you coming forward like this, Ms. Rennard."

Tears welled in her eyes. "I had to. My sister made her fair share of mistakes and God knew she wasn't perfect. But she didn't deserve to be killed."

"No, ma'am, she didn't. We'll do all we can to find the person responsible."

After Tess drove away, Jack ducked his head and headed back to his Jeep. Once inside with the heat blasting, he pulled out his notebook and wrote down their conversation. On the next page he wrote down *Mark Crandall, Dillon Ward* and *Young Lover.* Circled the last entry three times. Tess Rennard had given him another piece to the puzzle.

Now it was up to Jack to determine where that piece fit.

CHAPTER ELEVEN

KELSEY MADE HER WAY DOWN the bar, picking up empties and wiping the counter. A quick glance around the room satisfied her that everyone was taken care of. Since weeknights were slow, Allie allowed her lone waitress to end her shift when the kitchen closed at nine. Which left Kelsey alone to run the bar while Allie cleaned up the kitchen and did prep work for the next day's menu.

The Summit was a far cry from her previous place of employment. No flashing strobe lights, obscenely loud music or barely legal girls in tight, short skirts and tighter, shorter tops gyrating on the dance floor. Only soft lighting, classic rock on the jukebox and a blue collar clientele doing the world a favor by keeping their navels covered.

Funny how…comfortable it all was. Too bad comfortable didn't equate busy. Because that's what she needed—to keep busy. Otherwise her mind wandered, and it always strolled to the same place. Back to Jack and what happened between them two days ago.

She tossed the cleaning rag under the bar and poured herself a soda. Took a sip to ease the sudden dryness in her mouth. Oh, man, she had to stop thinking about Jack. And she really, really had to stop wanting him.

"Excuse me," a chubby, bespectacled blonde said as she lifted herself onto a stool, "but aren't you Kelsey Reagan? Dillon Ward's sister?"

Kelsey slowly lowered her glass. "Yeah. I'm Kelsey."

The woman bared her teeth in a predatory smile at odds with her soft, round face. "I'm Dora Wilkins with the *Serenity Springs Gazette*. I was wondering if I could ask you a few questions."

Kelsey blinked. Dora looked to be in her early forties, had wavy ash-blond hair cut in a chin-length bob and thin, severely arched eyebrows above burgundy, rectangular glasses. The tan sweatshirt she wore had a picture of a beagle puppy surrounded by colorful fall leaves.

She looked like a kindergarten teacher and so not how Kelsey had pictured the sludge-writing reporter. And it had nothing to do with Dora not having a forked tail and devil horns, either. Or at least, not much.

"I have nothing to say to you," Kelsey said.

Dora glanced up as she pulled a notebook and pen from her purse. "I'd have thought you'd want to comment. Seeing as how they're planning on arresting your brother for Shannon Crandall's murder—"

"Dillon is innocent." Kelsey grit out the words from between her teeth. "You can quote me on that."

"Be that as it may," Dora continued, "I have it on good authority the police now have enough evidence to arrest your brother and that this case will be wrapped up by the weekend."

Refusing to rise to the reporter's bait, she sipped her soda and hoped like hell she looked calm and collected. "Any evidence the police department thinks it has against Dillon is circumstantial."

"Hmm, yes, well, you'd be surprised how strong circumstantial evidence can be." She leaned forward, lowered her voice. "Besides, your brother killed once before. It's not really that much of a stretch to believe he's done it again."

Kelsey took a menacing step forward when someone laid a restraining hand on her arm. She swung around and faced Allie.

"I think Mike's ready for a refill," Allie said and nodded at a painfully thin man at the end of the bar. "Could you take care of that for me?"

Teeth ground together, hand still curled into a fist, she stalked to the end of the bar. Damn it, *damn it*. She had to get a grip. She couldn't let someone like Dora get under her skin.

After getting Mike another beer, she took a deep breath, counted to ten and let it out. She still felt the urge to break Dora's pointy nose, but she wouldn't. She could control herself. For Dillon.

Besides, what would Jack think if she ended up in his jail for assault?

Realizing she cared—too much—about what Jack thought about her, she frowned.

"…just doing my job," Dora was saying when Kelsey went back to Allie. "Gathering quotes for my story."

"Why not just make up the so-called quotes like you usually do?" Allie asked.

Dora blushed. "I can see freedom of the press is not an acceptable concept here at The Summit." She swiveled off the stool and shoved her notebook in her purse. "I'm sure my readers will be interested to learn how far you're willing to go to protect your…handyman."

Allie smiled thinly. "I bet that'll make for riveting copy.

And I'm just itching for the chance to sue you and the newspaper for libel."

"Before I leave, Allie perhaps you'd like to comment about your brother's problems in handling this case."

Allie stiffened. "Jack isn't having any problems—"

"Isn't he?" Dora's smug smile made the back of Kelsey's neck prickle. "City council has called an emergency meeting to take place as soon as possible."

"So?"

"Some of the council members feel your brother has bungled this investigation. And, since there have been rumors of impropriety on the chief's part, the council wants him to resign."

Kelsey felt sick. They were going to ask Jack to quit if he didn't arrest Dillon?

"Jack hasn't done anything wrong," Allie snapped. "Certainly nothing that would endanger his job."

"Hasn't he?" Dora asked, her gaze shifting to Kelsey. "As I said, the council's asking for his resignation. If they don't get it, they plan on asking the mayor to fire him."

JACK ZIPPED HIS JEANS as he hurried through the dark hallway to the kitchen. He flicked the back light on, unlocked the door and yanked it open.

"Kelsey?" He squeezed his eyes shut, but when he opened them again, she still stood on his deck, rain plastering her hair to her head. "Is something wrong? Are you hurt?"

"Could I come in?" she asked.

He opened the door wider to let her by and was immediately sprayed with freezing, blowing rain. Gooseflesh rose on his arms and chest and he wished he'd taken the time to put a shirt on.

He shut the door behind her. "Are you all right? Were you in an accident?"

"I'm fine."

He stepped forward. "Allie?"

"No. She's good. Everyone's okay." She pulled the strap of her purse higher up on her shoulder and pushed her wet hair out of her eyes. "Is it true you're going to arrest Dillon?"

His jaw dropped. "You can't be serious."

"Just answer the question, Jack."

"It's two-thirty in the morning."

Not only was it past the middle of the night, but it was also miserable out—windy and raining with temperatures barely above freezing. Which Kelsey could obviously attest to seeing as how she was soaked through. Water dripped from her hair and ran down her ashen face. Her lips were pale, her teeth were chattering and she was starting to shiver.

He rolled his eyes. He would never understand women.

"Yes or no," she said. "It's as simple—"

"Shh." He glanced through the doorway toward the stairs. Emma was usually a sound sleeper, had been dead to the world when he'd peeked in on her before coming downstairs, but he didn't want to chance waking her up. "Come on."

He wrapped his hand around Kelsey's upper arm. The material of her jacket was soggy and cold under his fingers. Surprised she willingly—and silently—followed him to the laundry room, he was able to flip on the overhead light and shut the door before she spoke again.

"You can't arrest Dillon. You have no evidence."

He wiped his hand down the side of his jeans and noticed a puddle forming on the tile floor beneath her. "Take your jacket off."

She opened her mouth. Shut it and frowned. "What?"

"You're soaked. Take it off."

She set her purse on the shelf behind her. While she struggled with the wet jacket, Jack reached into the dryer.

He tossed her a towel, which she caught with her free hand. She dropped her jacket onto the floor and rubbed the towel over her hair. The smell of her shampoo hit him like a right jab.

He watched as she gently mopped the moisture off her face before tipping her head back and patting her throat dry. Her wet jeans molded themselves to her long legs and slim hips and her bra and hard nipples were clearly outlined through her damp shirt.

God help him, he couldn't stop himself from ogling her like she was a contestant in a wet T-shirt contest and he was the final judge.

He forced his gaze up to her face and froze. She was staring at him, as intently as he'd been staring at her. Her gaze roamed over his bare shoulders and chest, down his torso to the unsnapped button of his jeans.

Her teeth sank into her luscious lower lip and Jack bit back a groan. Or maybe he didn't, because suddenly she raised her head and met his eyes. The narrow room—cramped with a washing machine and dryer along one wall, and floor-to-ceiling shelves and a built-in counter on the opposite side—seemed to shrink.

Jack clenched his teeth and shoved his hands into his pockets. Leaned back against the washing machine.

"Why did you go around back?" he asked. The porch's roof would've provided a bit of shelter from the pouring rain.

She looked away. "I didn't want anyone to see me."

"Because?"

"Because…that Dora person—"

"Dora Wilkins?" He straightened. "The reporter?"

"Yeah. She came into the bar tonight." Kelsey twisted the towel in her hands. "She said there was some new evidence and—"

"There is no new evidence." Forever championing her brother. "Dora was messing with you. Trying to get a reaction. Shannon's murder is still under full investigation."

"So, you're not going to arrest Dillon?"

There was a loaded question if he'd ever heard one. "I'm not going to arrest anyone. Yet." Relief filled her eyes and, not for the first time, he hoped her faith in her brother wasn't wasted. "I'm not going to lie to you, Ward is still a suspect."

"No," she said thoughtfully, "you wouldn't lie." She stepped toward him and damn if that washer wasn't right behind him, he would've backed up. "But will you still do what's right? No matter what?"

He took the mangled towel from her hands and tossed it on a pile of dirty clothes. "I'll do my job, honestly and fairly."

"You might not get the chance. The city council is calling some special meeting. They're going to ask for your resignation, Jack."

He slapped the top of the washing machine. "They won't get it."

"Then they'll fire you. Or get the mayor to do it."

"She can't. Not on her own," he amended. He rubbed the back of his neck. Damn, what a disaster. "Besides the mayor's agreement, they need a two-thirds majority vote from council to terminate my contract."

"What if that happens?"

"It won't." While Mark Crandall—and Jack had no doubt Mark was the one behind all of this—had enough influence to call an unscheduled meeting, he didn't have enough backing on the council to fire Jack.

"What if it does?" Kelsey insisted. "Are you going to cave under the pressure and throw my brother to the wolves to save your own skin?"

His head snapped back as if she'd sucker punched him. "Do you really think so little of me?"

"I'm sorry, okay?" she said and grabbed his arm when he would've turned away. "I'm just…the reporter freaked me out. I know she meant to and it pisses me off that it worked, but I can't help it." She raised her hand beseechingly. "Look, I know you're a good cop, an honest one. I'm just not…used to trusting anyone. This is new territory for me."

Jack wanted to hang on to his anger—damn it, he had a right to be angry and to stay that way. But as he looked at Kelsey, saw the vulnerability in her eyes, saw the open honesty on her face, he felt his anger melting away.

He sighed. He was such a sap. "When I give my word, I keep it. You can count on that."

"I want to," she admitted quietly as she laid a hand on his chest. His heart skipped a beat under her fingers. "It scares me how much I want to believe you, to count on you."

He cleared his throat and stepped back so that her fingers trailed a path of heat down his torso as her hand slid away. "Why don't you finish drying off? I'll go upstairs and grab you some dry clothes, then we can—"

Talk.

Except he never got that last word out. He couldn't. Not with Kelsey's lips on his.

She'd lunged at him, wrapped her arms around his neck and fused her mouth to his. The force of her movement knocked him back against the washing machine with a soft thud.

Her lips were soft and cold, but warming quickly thanks to their frenzied movement over his. Her tongue swept into his mouth, shy at first, then growing bolder. She smelled like rain and cold mountain air, and God help him, he couldn't resist her. He plunged his hands in her wet hair while he angled his head to take control of the kiss, to take it deeper.

He could hardly believe this was happening.

Wait a minute…was this happening?

Kelsey felt real enough in his arms, though quite a bit colder and damper than in his dreams. The most recent being fifteen minutes ago when her pounding on the door had awakened him.

Maybe that's why he laid his hands on her shoulders and set her away from him. Because he was having a hard time separating fact from fantasy. Because, for the life of him, he couldn't figure out why Kelsey would suddenly throw herself at him.

Because he was a complete idiot.

"Hold on," Jack managed to say when she attempted to kiss him again. "What's going on here?"

"Well, if it isn't obvious, then I'm not doing it right."

Her voice was a low, husky purr.

"If you did it any righter, I'd embarrass myself."

She smiled up at him. "So what's the problem?"

The problem was she was caressing his chest, her fingertips stroking over his nipples, her fingernails scraping his skin, making it difficult for him to gather his thoughts. He reached down, grabbed her wrists and held her hands away from his body. "Why the change of heart, Kelsey? A few days ago, you didn't want this."

Her fingers curled. "I did want it," she said hesitantly, "I just wasn't sure it was the best thing for either of us."

"And now?"

She exhaled heavily. "Now I'm more certain than ever that us getting together is a mistake. But I don't care." She lifted her chin, her eyes dark and steady on his. "I want to be with you, Jack."

DIDN'T HE WANT HER? She'd just bared her heart to him, as much as she was able, yet he still held her at arm's length. Literally.

Well, seeing as how she'd already gone this far, she might as well go for broke. She rose up and settled her mouth on his. Again she tasted his surprise, his resistance. She wanted him to return her kiss, to touch her, to want her like he had the other day.

She needed him. Now. Right now. Needed to have something real and honorable in her life, just this once. If he turned her away, she might never get another opportunity.

She put her heart and soul into the kiss, everything she couldn't say, hoping he'd understand what she wanted, what she needed. He dropped his hold of her, his hands going to her waist. His fingers bit into her hips. She touched him, ran her hands over his smooth, taut skin, thrilled to know she could cause his muscles to flex and bunch with a simple touch.

With a low, guttural groan, Jack took over the kiss—and surrendered his resistance. He lifted her and turned so that her back pressed against the washing machine. She wrapped her legs around his hips.

One hand at her neck, he nudged her head back as he ran his lips across her jawbone and down her exposed throat. She smoothed her hands over his shoulders, across his upper back while he placed hot, wet, openmouthed kisses on her neck. He nipped at her pulse and she caught her breath then released it on a raspy moan when he soothed the sting with his tongue.

Jack eased back enough to draw her shirt up under her arms. With a quick flick, he undid her bra, spread the cups aside and lowered his head.

His mouth was hot against her cool skin, the way he licked and suckled her sensitive breasts incredibly arousing. She slid her hands into his hair as if to hold him there, right there, so he couldn't stop his sweet torture. Her need for him grew, expanded until she was afraid it would completely take over. Take over her mind. Her senses. Her control.

And her heart.

She squeezed her eyes shut. No, she couldn't allow this…longing for Jack to mean anything. It was sex. Pure, simple, basic. And all someone like her had the right to expect from a man as good and decent as him.

She reached between them, found the tab of his zipper and tugged it down.

He suddenly stepped back. "Kelsey, maybe we should slow down."

He wasn't going to stop them. Not after she'd convinced herself she could share her body with him and keep her heart separate.

"You think so?" she asked lowly as she slid her hand inside his briefs and cupped him. "I kind of like this speed."

He shut his eyes and hissed out a breath between his teeth. Kelsey wrapped her hand around him. He was hot and hard and obviously no more interested in stopping than she was.

She stroked him, learning his shape and length, the weight of him. "I don't want to slow down," she told him as she stared into his eyes. "I don't want to wonder if this is a mistake or worry about what's going to happen tomorrow. I just want to feel you inside of me. Now."

His eyes smoldered and then he was kissing her again as he worked to pull her wet jeans down her legs. When her pants and panties were around her ankles, he slid a knee between her legs and eased her thighs apart.

With his tongue stroking inside her mouth, he waited at her entrance. Her body instinctively rocked toward him, his heat, his hardness. He began to slide inside her when she slapped her hands against his chest and pulled her head back.

"Wait," she gasped. "Condom."

Jack swore. His body shook and sweat beaded on his upper lip. And though she tried to fight it, Kelsey's heart melted that he'd not only stopped when she'd asked him, but at the effort it took him to restrain himself.

"Upstairs," he ground out.

"No." She reached behind him, grabbed her purse and dug through it. When she found what she was looking for, she dropped the purse onto the floor and held her hand up so Jack could see the square, foil packet.

He kissed her, a slow and sweet I'm-so-damn-happy-you're-prepared kiss. He took the condom from her, ripped it open and covered himself. With his eyes, dark and intense, on hers, he entered her in one smooth stroke.

Having Jack moving inside her was so much more than

she'd dreamed. It wasn't just good, wasn't just right. It felt…complete. Made her feel complete.

Startled at her own thoughts, at her reaction to what was supposed to have been just sex—what she *needed* to be just sex—she squeezed her eyes shut.

"Look at me," Jack demanded in a low murmur, cupping her face in both hands. She shook her head, but when he withdrew from her almost completely, her eyes opened on their own accord. "That's right. Just keep looking at me."

He pushed back into her slowly. With each deliberate thrust, tension grew and coiled inside her until she wanted release more than she wanted her next breath. Rising onto her toes, she gripped his shoulders and moved her hips in an attempt to somehow get closer to him, to ease the ache between her legs.

Her fingers dug into his flesh. Breathy, short moans escaped her. Jack grabbed her hips and drove into her faster and faster, left her gasping. Had her spiraling toward climax. She cried out hoarsely as she came, her body shaking from the power of her orgasm. As she trembled with delicious aftershocks, she was vaguely aware of Jack shuddering with his own release.

He withdrew from her and she fell back against the machine. He rested his forehead against hers, his breathing still fast and choppy. The room smelled like rain, sweat and sex. She inhaled deeply, trying to chisel this experience—the smell, taste and especially the feel of Jack—into her memory.

He lifted his head and his smile warmed her. Made her panic. "Wow," she blurted, "me coming over here worked out better than I thought."

Jack cursed softly, pushed away and turned his back to her as he yanked up his pants.

Frowning, she readjusted her bra and shirt and pulled on her panties. "What's wrong?"

"Nothing." He clenched his hands at his sides. "Except we just had sex while my daughter's sleeping upstairs."

She blanched. Jeez, she hadn't thought about the little girl. She glanced at the door, relieved to find it still firmly shut. Thank God she didn't have to add corrupting impressionable kids to her long list of sins.

"Did you plan this?"

She jerked her gaze back to Jack. "What?"

"Was this—" he gestured between them "—a setup? A way for you to gain leverage over me?" His eyes were like chips of blue ice, his voice as frigid as the wind outside.

Tears clogged her throat. Not *again*. She viciously swallowed them back. God, she was such an idiot, she thought savagely as she attempted to wrestle back into her jeans. So stupid. For a moment she'd actually thought what they'd just shared had been special. That it had meant something.

She'd just made yet another impulsive, asinine mistake. Dillon had been right about her. She really hadn't changed and probably never would.

She wrenched her jeans over her hips and fastened them. Without looking Jack's way, she snatched her jacket off the floor and opened the door.

"Hold on a minute." He grabbed her by the arm and spun her to face him.

She yanked her arm free. "I have nothing to say. You have it all figured out."

"What am I supposed to think? You're the one who told me you'd do anything for your brother."

"That's right, I did. But what happened here just now

wasn't one-sided. You weren't exactly fighting me off. And remember, you're the one who said once would get me out of your system." She hated, *hated,* that her voice shook. That her heart was breaking. "I hope like hell it worked."

CHAPTER TWELVE

JACK WALKED INTO THE SUMMIT the next morning and knew his day had gone from bad to complete and utter hell.

"I've had it with small-town cops," Kelsey warned Ben Michaels as she stood between him and her brother. "Small-minded, small-town cops in particular. So, I suggest you go on your merry way." She waved the pool cue she held like a club. "Unless you want a real stick shoved up your—"

"Is there a problem here, Michaels?" Jack asked in a fairly impassive tone.

Impassive tone or not, Kelsey glared at him like some sort of fierce, pixie warrior.

"Chief, I'm glad you're here," Michaels said unsteadily. "She's crazy."

"I'll show you crazy," Kelsey promised and stepped forward.

He really didn't need this. Jack stalked over to Kelsey and, after a brief tug-of-war, jerked the cue out of her hands and tossed it onto the pool table.

"Now, what in the hell is going on?"

Kelsey crossed her arms. "Mini-cop over there is harassing my brother."

Michaels's face turned crimson. "I was checking on Mr. Ward's whereabouts."

"Well, you can clearly see he's still here," Kelsey said. "Guess that means you're free to go."

Ward touched Kelsey's arm and spoke directly into her ear. She gave an ill-natured shrug and then stomped off to stand behind the bar.

Ward watched his sister walk away before turning to look at Jack with hard, flat eyes. "If you have everything under control, mind if I get back to work?"

Though Jack doubted Ward really was asking for his permission, he nodded anyway, and waited for the other man to disappear into the kitchen before motioning Michaels over.

"Officer Michaels," Jack said, "didn't your shift end over two hours ago?"

"No. I mean…yes. I mean, I'm on third shift."

"And yet, here you are, not only still in full uniform, but also disobeying my direct order not to confront Ward."

"I told you," Michaels said petulantly, "I was checking to make sure he hadn't skipped town."

"Officer Harden is on duty at this time with orders—" he stressed the last word so the kid couldn't miss his meaning "—to report Ward's whereabouts."

"We wouldn't have to waste our time following him around if we'd just arrest him," Michaels mumbled.

Jack stepped forward. The kid was smart enough to scurry backward until he bumped into the door. "I'm still police chief here, which means I'm still in charge of this investigation."

Michaels lifted his chin. "Not for long."

Jack held Michaels's gaze until the cockiness disappeared from the kid's eyes and he looked away. "Long enough to tell you that if you disobey a direct order again, you'll face a suspension of duty. As it is, I'm issuing you an official reprimand for the stunt you pulled here today."

Michaels blanched but recovered faster than Jack would've expected. "What about her?" He jerked his head in Kelsey's direction. "She threatened to assault me."

"I'll handle it."

"Sure you will," Michaels said, sneering.

"I said, I'd take care of it." At the quiet authority in Jack's voice, Michaels swallowed and averted his gaze. Keeping his eyes on the kid, Jack opened the door. "Whether you like it, I'm still the officer in charge. You might want to remember that."

Michaels stiffened, nodded abruptly then stormed off. The door slammed in Jack's face with a resounding bang.

"That idiot is a one-man gestapo," Kelsey called.

The pounding in his head intensified as he crossed back to the bar. "Michaels won't bother you or your brother again."

"Good." Kelsey turned and presented her rigid back to him.

"We need to talk."

"I have nothing to say."

"Then you can listen."

"Not interested."

"Don't push me, Kelsey," he warned.

She looked over her shoulder. "I wouldn't dream of it."

But she'd already pushed him, hadn't she? She'd pushed him until he'd lost control. Until he'd gone against the instincts that told him he couldn't, *shouldn't* get involved with her.

"I want—"

"It's past time you learned, you don't always get what you want."

"I realize I probably didn't handle the situation as well as I could have—"

"You mean you don't always make the women you have sex with feel cheap and dirty?"

He'd expected her bitterness, knew he deserved it and possibly worse. What he hadn't expected was the slight, almost undetectable tremble in her voice. The hint of dejection and humiliation in her eyes.

Or that he'd want to do whatever it took, say whatever he needed to say, to make that pain disappear.

"I never meant to hurt you, Kelsey."

"You didn't," she said quickly, looking away. "We both know last night was a mistake. You want to lay the blame at my feet? Fine. I accept full responsibility. Feel better?"

Hell no, he didn't feel better. "All I want is a chance to explain why I said what I did last night."

"No explanation necessary," she said as she walked around to the front of the bar. "You made it quite clear what you think of me."

When she would have walked past him, he stepped in front of her. "We have to talk about it sometime."

She looked him dead in the eye. "I'd rather walk through hell barefoot, naked and doused in gasoline."

She neatly sidestepped him and stormed off. Frustrated, he moved to go after her when Ward's voice stopped him.

"I wouldn't do that if I were you."

Jack swore and turned to see Ward lounging in the kitchen doorway. "Do what?"

"Chase after her. When Kelsey gets a mad going, the best thing to do is wait it out," Ward said. "I know my sister. She's impulsive, rash and rude. Her temper is quick to flare and slow to die down. And when she gets mad, she gets mean."

"Thanks for the insight, but—"

"She's also smart," Ward continued as if Jack hadn't spoken. "Smarter than even she realizes. She has a wicked sense of humor, is a whiz with numbers and is loyal to a fault. She's cautious with her heart, but once she cares about someone, she sticks with them through thick and thin."

"I know all I need to know about Kelsey," Jack said in exasperation. "So if you have something to say, spit it out."

Ward straightened, his face expressionless, his voice cool. "Kelsey puts on a decent show but she's not as tough as she acts. And if you hurt her, you're going to answer to me."

THE SCENT OF SAUTÉED ONIONS and peppers, along with the low hum of voices and music from the bar, met Kelsey as she descended the back stairs into The Summit's kitchen. Spotting Allie at the stove, she stepped off the lowest stair only to be waylaid by a child's joyful cry. Before she could evade Emma, the girl flew across the room and attached herself to Kelsey's leg.

"Uh, hey there, kid. What are you doing here?" she asked, awkwardly patting Emma's head. She searched the large room. "Your dad's not here is he?"

Emma grinned. "Daddy had to work late so Aunt Allie's babysitting."

"Thank God." The last thing she wanted was to go another round with the police chief. "Maybe my luck's about to change."

Emma pulled back, her face scrunched into a frown. "Huh?"

"I said, uh, isn't that a lucky change?"

Emma rewarded her quick thinking with a big smile and finally let go of Kelsey's legs.

"I didn't realize you two knew each other," Allie said, watching them intently.

"Kelsey helped me and Daddy make cookies." Emma tugged on Kelsey's hand and pulled her over to the large table. "Daddy made some and they were yucky, but Kelsey's were real good and you don't even bake them," she continued as she climbed onto a chair. "You just mix some stuff and plop them down."

"Oh, really?" Allie raised her eyebrows.

"Look, Kelsey." Emma, standing on her chair, shoved her hands in Kelsey's face. "Daddy did my nails last night."

"Oh…ahh…" She tried to focus on Emma's tiny, pink nails, ignoring the sweet image of Jack painting his daughter's nails. "Those are—"

"And I'm gonna spend the night at Hayley's Saturday and her mom's gonna put makeup on us and do our hair real fancy and we're going to rent a movie and make homemade pizza and stay up real late, maybe even midnight."

Kelsey blinked. "Well, that uh, sounds like—"

"And," Emma continued, barely pausing for a breath, "today we learned what to do if there's a 'mergency, like if your grandma is choking on a grape or there's a fire or if a bad man has a gun. Then we had a practice spelling test and I missed two words but Aunt Allie said if I got a hundred on the test tomorrow she'll take me for ice cream. The words are real hard 'cuz I'm in first grade but I've been studying them every night." She jumped off her seat. "I have the list in my backpack, wanna see it?"

"How about you wash your hands and eat your dinner first?" Allie suggested. "Then you can show Kelsey your spelling."

"Okay," Emma agreed as she skipped out of the room.

Dazed, Kelsey asked, "Do they serve that kid speed for lunch or what?"

"She's always wound up after school." Allie expertly flipped a chicken breast on the stove-top grill and glanced at Kelsey. "You look tired. What's the matter? Did you and Dillon have another argument?"

"Hard to argue with someone who barely speaks to you," she said. She knew she had clear signs of a sleepless night— dark circles, puffy red-rimmed eyes, pale complexion—she didn't need to be told she looked awful. Kelsey grabbed a slice of raw pepper and popped it into her mouth. "Even when I try to pick a fight with Dillon he doesn't take the bait."

"What is it then?"

"Nothing. Everything's fine. I didn't sleep well last night, that's all."

"Uh-huh," Allie said. "Funny how you and Jack didn't say anything about making cookies."

"Not much to mention. You know, I really am beat," she said, adding a totally fake yawn for effect. "I think I'll just eat upstairs, maybe read a bit and call it an early night."

"Fine. Don't tell me what's going on between you and Jack." Allie laid a fresh roll on a baking sheet and slid it into the oven. "I'll just allow my imagination to fill in the blanks."

"It's no big deal. I went over to Jack's house a few nights ago to talk to him about Dillon. When I got there, he and the kid were having a slight problem and I helped them out."

"So you and Jack have gotten past your apprehension toward each other?"

Kelsey, in the act of eating another slice of pepper, choked. Eyes watering, she coughed and cleared her throat. "I'd say we're past the apprehension stage all right."

Yeah, she and Jack had moved beyond apprehension and on to hostility. At the rate they were going, they'd be at full-blown animosity by the end of the day.

Allie took the rolls out of the oven, placed a chicken breast on each one and topped them with thin slices of mozzarella cheese. "That's great. And it was so nice of you to help him out that way. Especially with all that's going on."

Kelsey's face grew warm. "I wasn't helping Jack so much as Emma."

Who would be returning with her nonstop chatter any minute now. If that wasn't reason enough to escape, she didn't know what was.

"Look, I'll just come back later, okay?" Kelsey backed up a step. "When you're not so busy."

Emma rushed back into the room at the same time the waitress came in from the bar and dropped off a meal order.

Allie read the order slip. "Don't you want something to eat?" she asked Kelsey. "After I take care of this, I can fix you something."

"Don't bother. I have some food upstairs. I'll just make myself a sandwich."

Emma tugged on Kelsey's jeans. "Are you going upstairs? Can I go, too? Please? *Please?*" she begged, looking up at her with pure adoration.

Okay, so the kid made her heart melt a little. She wasn't totally unfeeling.

Kelsey felt Allie's eyes on her. She sighed. No way could she turn the kid down. "If it's okay with your aunt."

"Can I, Aunt Allie?"

"I don't see why not," Allie said.

Emma squealed in delight and ran across the room to grab her backpack off a bench by the door. She raced for the stairs. "Come on, Kelsey."

Kelsey tore her gaze away from Emma's retreating figure to find Allie staring at her, one dark eyebrow raised, her blue eyes filled with curiosity.

Jeez, it was a good thing she had put Jack out of her mind for good. Otherwise, she might have to admit how much Allie resembled her brother at the moment. Freaky.

"Are you sure there's nothing going on between you and Jack?" Allie asked in an undertone.

Talk about a loaded question. Kelsey met Allie's gaze head-on. And told her the only thing she was absolutely sure of. "There is nothing, and I mean nothing, going on between me and Jack."

The look on Allie's face said she didn't believe it. Well, that was just too damn bad. Oh, maybe there had been a tiny, little something going on between them, but that was over. Done.

After the way he'd hurt her, Kelsey would do anything, and everything, in her power to keep it that way. Hey, mistakes happened—don't dwell on them. Better yet, pretend they didn't happen at all and forget about them completely.

But just because she was becoming an expert at forgetting her mistakes didn't mean she couldn't learn from them. She'd learned a doozy last night. She needed to stay far away from Jack Martin.

JACK SLID ONTO A STOOL at the end of the bar and watched Luke Erickson, the only other patron still at The Summit, smile at Kelsey. Whatever the ski bum was saying made her grin. Jack clenched his hands.

Kelsey could handle herself. She'd proved it these past few days. She hadn't had any problem ignoring or avoiding him had she?

She wouldn't have any problems handling a kid like Luke, either. Even if he was single, good-looking and had more money than brains. If Luke went too far, she'd cut him down to size with that sharp tongue of hers.

When Luke reached out and laid his hand on Kelsey's arm, Jack narrowed his eyes. His vision blurred when—instead of biting the kid's hand off—she smiled at him.

Kelsey laughed at something the ski bum said and Jack got to his feet. He moved down a few stools so that Kelsey would have to speak to him. Acknowledge him.

Though she only had eyes for Luke, she visibly stiffened when Jack sat down. "We've already had last call, Sheriff."

"I know." He kept his voice even. "I'll just have a soda."

She frowned but got his drink and set it on a paper napkin in front of him all without so much as glancing his way.

"Hey, Jack," Luke said as Kelsey went to wipe down the other end of the bar.

Jack nodded.

"Does she know you're the chief and not the sheriff?" Luke asked him.

"She knows. She just says it to tick me off."

Luke grinned but wisely kept from saying how it seemed to be working.

Jack picked up his drink and moved down a few more stools to sit next to Luke. He sipped his drink. "Weather's turning," he commented mildly. "We're due for some freezing rain. You should head out before it starts."

Luke looked from Jack to Kelsey and back, before sighing heavily and standing up. Despite his pretty looks, Luke was brighter than Jack had given him credit for.

"I guess I'll be going," Luke told Kelsey. *That's right, kid, move along.* "Thanks for the beer."

Kelsey smiled again and Jack wanted to wring Luke's neck. "That's what I'm here for," she said.

Luke walked out the door leaving Jack and Kelsey alone. After a slow, burning eternity in hell—at least that's how it felt to Jack—she returned to stand in front of him.

"We're closing," she told him flatly.

He leaned across the bar and caught her by the wrist. "I really blew it, didn't I?"

She attempted to pull away but he wouldn't let her. "I don't know what you're talking about."

"Kelsey, you can't avoid me forever—"

"Wanna bet?" When she tugged away this time, he let go. She took a hasty step back.

Out of the corner of his eye, he saw Allie approaching them. He got to his feet. "Come with me," he urged lowly. "We can grab a cup of coffee. If I could just—"

Allie went behind the bar. "No hassling the bartender."

He kept his gaze on Kelsey. "I wasn't hassling her."

"I don't have time for this," Kelsey said. "I have to help Allie clean up and—"

"I'll help."

"What?" Kelsey asked at the same time Allie said, "Excuse me?"

"I said, I'll help you clean up."

"I don't need your help." Kelsey slapped the cloth onto the bar. She grabbed a tray of empties and stormed through the doors to the kitchen.

"What was that all about?" Allie asked.

He shook his head. "Nothing."

"Oh, no, you don't. That was definitely not nothing." She crossed her arms. "That was something. What did you do to her?"

"Kelsey and I had a...misunderstanding."

"Uh-huh. The next thing you're going to tell me is that there's nothing going on between the two of you. That you and Kelsey are just friends."

"No. I'm not going to try and tell you that." Any man would be crazy to want to be *just friends* with someone as sexy and desirable as Kelsey. "I can't get into it so you're just going to have to trust me here, Allie." When she opened her mouth—no doubt to argue with him—he added, "Please."

She dropped her arms. "Fine, but remember, there's a lot at stake here."

"Besides Ward's freedom?"

"Dillon's innocent. I have faith he'll be fine."

"Then what are you so worried about?"

"I know about the problems Mark Crandall is causing with city council, Jack. He wants you to resign—"

"That's not going to happen."

She rolled her eyes. "Obviously, as you're no quitter and don't respond to being bullied." She lowered her voice. "But, as much as I like Kelsey, I don't think it's very smart for you to get involved with her. At least not until Dillon is cleared."

"I appreciate your concern, but I've got everything under control."

Besides, Allie's advice came too late. He and Kelsey were already involved. Whether Kelsey admitted it or not.

CHAPTER THIRTEEN

JACK WASN'T LEAVING. Not on his own, anyway. And unfortunately, Kelsey wasn't strong enough to put him in a headlock and drag him to the door.

She walked into the bar and, as she'd done for the past half hour, studiously ignored him. He didn't seem to mind, just continued stacking chairs onto tables for them to sweep and mop the floor in the morning.

He was only helping clean so Allie would be done sooner and leave.

"I'm done," Allie said, putting on her jacket. "And not a moment too soon. I'm beginning to suffocate from all the tension in here."

Jack looked up. "I'll walk you out."

"I'm parked out front—"

"Then I won't have far to go." He took Allie's elbow, glanced at Kelsey. "I'll be right back."

That's what she was afraid of. As soon as the door shut behind him, Kelsey raced over and defiantly flipped the dead bolt, grinning at the loud click it made as it locked.

Releasing a long breath, she headed down the hall to the small stock room. Usually she would wait until the next day to restock the liquor, but she was too keyed up to go to bed.

After finding an empty wine crate and filling it with what she needed, she used her hip to push the door closed, walked back into the bar, and almost dropped the bottles on the floor.

Jack—of the catlike reflexes—grabbed the box from her. "I've got it," he said as he took the heavy crate and set it on the bar.

"Isn't breaking and entering high up on your list of no-no's?"

"Allie loaned me the key."

"That traitor," she mumbled. "So much for sisterhood."

"I never would've pegged you as a coward, Kelsey."

She stepped behind the bar and lifted a bottle of vodka out of the crate. "Look, it's late and I'm tired, so just…say what you have to say."

"Fair enough." He leaned against the bar. She could feel his gaze on her as she unloaded bottles and placed them on the shelves. "First of all, I want to thank you for watching Emma the other day."

Heat suffused her face. "It wasn't a big deal."

And it hadn't been. It hadn't even been *all* that bad. The kid was okay company—even if she was a motormouth.

"It was a big deal to Emma," he said. "She hasn't stopped talking about it. How you helped her with her spelling and made her dinner."

Surprised—and okay, maybe a bit pleased—she turned and met his warm gaze. She immediately turned her back to him again. "All I did was recite a few words to her and slap together a peanut butter and jelly sandwich."

"According to Emma, it was the best sandwich she's ever had." She didn't respond and Jack sighed. "I shouldn't have acted the way I did the other night. I shouldn't have said what I said."

She cleared her throat but kept her back to him. She needed to say something, but what? You hurt me? Yeah, right. Why didn't she just hand her heart over to him to stomp on while she was at it?

"I'm sorry," he said softly, his voice close. Too close. She whirled around and found herself nose to chest with him.

Before she could move away, Jack lifted her onto her toes, pulled her forward until their faces were only inches apart. "I was wrong and that bothers me. But one time with you wasn't nearly enough," he said, an edge to his voice, "and I can't see you without wanting to do this."

This was a deep, tongue-tangling kiss. Reason faded from her mind as his kiss slowed to something smooth and sweet. She grabbed on to his shoulders. And kissed him back.

Oh, God. She could refuse him nothing.

He suddenly broke the kiss, let go of his hold on her and stepped back. Kelsey fell back on her heels.

She snatched her half-empty bottle of water from under the counter and drained it in three, thirsty gulps.

God, she was so stupid. By sharing her body with him, she'd inadvertently given a piece of herself away.

A piece she desperately wanted back.

"Just go, Jack," she said, hating the pleading note in her voice. "Leave this be." Leave *her* be.

"I can't," he said quietly.

"Because you want a repeat performance of the other night," she said, confused by the warmth in his expression and the tightness of his jaw.

"No, damn it. Because I care about you."

KELSEY'S FACE DRAINED OF COLOR. Jack's stomach, along with his ego, took a nosedive. He shoved his hands in his pockets and waited, hoping like hell she believed him, that she trusted him.

"You don't have to say that." She edged around him, something pretty damn close to panic in her eyes. "We already had sex."

"I didn't say it to get laid." Fighting to keep his voice calm, he followed her out from behind the bar. "I said it because it's true. I'm sorry about the other night. Making love to you that way…with Emma sleeping upstairs—"

"It never occurred to me," she blurted. "About Emma. That she could come downstairs and…find us…like that. I wouldn't want to, you know, freak her out or anything."

"I know that. But with all that's going on with the investigation and your brother, you have to admit, it's not such a stretch for me to think you'd used me."

His chest tightened when she didn't deny it or defend herself. Normally he wouldn't complain about an incredibly hot woman using him solely for sex, but this was different.

She was different.

And though he had the mayor and city council raining threats on him, and his job was on the line, he wasn't ready to let Kelsey go.

"Even thinking you were using me," he continued, "I couldn't stop myself. I lost control and I took it out on you. If you didn't sleep with me to get me to help your brother—"

"I didn't." She tugged both hands through her hair. "God."

"Then why?"

She opened her mouth only to snap it shut again. Shook

her head. "It doesn't matter." She turned and walked over to the far end of the pool table.

"It matters to me."

"You won't believe me, anyway," she said, dropping her gaze.

"Kelsey, help me out here. I'm trying. And I'm not saying I don't have my share of blame in this. I was wrong to react that way, but when you said things worked out better than you thought they would, I jumped to conclusions."

"I didn't mean it like that."

"I know that now." Crossing to stand on the opposite side of the pool table, he rolled his shoulders but the tension tightening his muscles remained. "I want to know what's going on. And if I can, I want to help you."

She slid the eight ball across the felt top. It hit another ball with a sharp crack. "I really did go over to see if what that reporter said was true."

"You believed I'd arrest Ward to save my job?" Why was it she had complete faith in her brother and none in him?

"I didn't want to, but as the night wore on, I kept going over in my head what that reporter said and I realized…"

"Realized what?"

She gripped the edge of the table. "I realized I wouldn't blame you if you did."

"I would."

"Yeah, I know. I don't know many people like you, Jack. Honest and honorable. Most men, most cops in your situation, would take what they want and not care about what was right. They'd do what they needed to save their own ass. But you… You're different."

"But you still weren't sure."

"No. I wasn't. Or maybe I was and I needed to reassure myself. I don't know. At the time, all I knew was that you were in trouble."

He frowned. "Don't you mean Dillon was in trouble?"

"That's what I said."

"No, you said you thought I was in trouble."

She blushed. Averted her eyes. "Dillon. I meant Dillon."

"Kelsey," he asked, suspicion niggling in his brain, "were you worried about me?"

"I don't see what that has to do with anything."

He walked around the pool table, stopping directly in front of her. "Did you come over to my house because you were worried about your brother or me?"

She crossed her arms, her mouth set in a stubborn line. "Both."

"Then why the kiss?" *Why did you say those things to me?*

She hesitated. "That day here, when we moved tables, when you told me about what happened with that kid after your wife died—"

"You felt sorry for me." His stomach sank. Pity sex was worse than being used.

Her eyes flashed. "What are you, stupid?"

He pulled his shoulders back. "Hey—"

"You have everything. A beautiful daughter—" she said and jabbed her finger into his chest "—family and friends who love you—" jab, jab "—the respect of an entire town—" long, painful jab "—don't be an idiot. Of course I didn't feel sorry for you."

He eyed her warily and rubbed his chest. "Then why?"

"Because I wanted to be with someone like you," she said, her voice rising. "For once, I wanted to be with someone who was good and solid and strong. Someone who wasn't using *me*. You're so damn decent, too decent for someone like me. So, no," she said, her voice now barely a whisper. "I didn't use you. Or maybe I did, but not how you think. I...I wanted something good in my life. Just once, I wanted something good."

Jack exhaled heavily and realized the pain in his chest wasn't caused by Kelsey's finger. He'd been holding his breath. Holy God, he'd never been so happy to have been so off base before.

He opened his mouth, snapped it shut. Hell, if he was going to do this, he was going to do it right. Her eyes widened when he took both of her hands in his. He supposed it was a small victory she didn't try to pull away.

"You threw me for a loop that night. To be honest, you've been throwing me since the first day I met you." And why that didn't make him wash his hands of her, he wasn't sure. "I don't know what it is about you that makes me so crazy, but I never meant to hurt you."

"Well, since we're having this lovefest and all, I guess I'm sorry, too. For bulldozing you that way the other night." She tugged on her hands and when he released her, she stepped back. "But none of this matters."

"What if we want it to change?"

She looked startled and, for a half second, tempted. Then her chin came up. "Your job and my brother's freedom are on the line. Do you really think hot sex is worth the risk?"

He was afraid what they had was way more than just sex. And that there was way more at risk than just his job. Like his and Emma's hearts. "My job's secure." For the time being. "What about you?"

"What about me?"

"Have you considered what will happen, what you'll do if Ward is guilty of Shannon's murder?"

She took another step back. "He's not."

"You have to at least consider the possibility," he said gently. "Ward's changed. He's not the same person you remember."

"You don't understand. I want him to be the same." Her eyes filled with tears. "I need him to be."

"Maybe if you told me what happened that night, the night your stepfather was killed, I could understand." She shook her head. "Trust me, Kelsey. I can help you."

She wiped at her eyes. "You can't. You can't even understand. I've watched you—you and Emma and Allie. You're all so…" She twisted her fingers together and paused as if searching for the right word. "In tune with each other. You and Emma are surrounded by family and friends, people you can count on and turn to. People you can trust."

"All you had was Dillon."

"He was the one who went over my spelling words with me, who made sure I was fed and clothed and bathed. He was the one and only person in my life who truly cared about me."

"I get that, I do." Once again he reached for her hands. "But, for whatever reason, Dillon isn't the same kid who taught you to make cookies."

He was surprised when she linked her fingers through his and squeezed. "I know that."

Jack rubbed his thumbs over the soft, fragile skin on the backs of her hands. "I know you love your brother, and I know you think you owe him—"

"I do owe him," she said fiercely. "He saved my life that

night. He stopped Glenn from—" She broke off and pressed her lips together.

His stomach churned sickeningly. He already suspected what happened that night but he had to be sure. "What, Kelsey? He stopped your stepfather from hitting you? Beating you?"

She pulled away and hugged her arms around herself, her expression bleak. "He stopped that bastard from raping me."

KELSEY TURNED AWAY FROM the sympathy in Jack's eyes. "Now you see why I owe him?"

"Why didn't Ward's attorney bring this up in court?"

She slowly walked around the table, her fingers trailing the wooden edge. "I told you, he didn't think the judge would believe me."

"Why not?"

She stopped. "Because of the number of times I was in trouble with the police. That's why his attorney didn't believe me, why a judge wouldn't believe me. I'm the reason Glenn was in our lives to begin with. He met my mother after he'd picked me up for shoplifting when I was ten. Six months later they were married."

"None of that is your fault, Kelsey."

"Yeah, it was. Even knowing that a skipped class would get me a black eye or a smart-ass comeback would get me a split lip, I kept getting into trouble. Kept needing Dillon to protect me, to bail me out again and again." A lump formed in her throat and she swallowed. "I was the one who pissed Glenn off that night."

"You are not to blame for what Glenn tried to do to you. You were just a kid."

His defense of her made the damn lump grow. "But I knew better than to push him."

"What happened?" This time, his gentle tone didn't irritate her. Instead, it made her feel safe. And decidedly weepy.

Could she tell him? After she'd told Dillon's attorney the truth and he hadn't believed her, she'd never told another soul about that night. Had never wanted to tell anyone.

Until now.

"Glenn played softball a couple times a week with some of his cop buddies." She spoke hesitantly, unsure of where exactly to begin. "That night he and a few of his teammates were at the house drinking when I came home. I tried to ignore them but Glenn got in my face about my ditching a few classes that day." She cleared her throat and began circling the pool table again. "I…God, I don't know why but I just exploded. Told him to kiss ass in front of all his friends. I could actually see him fighting for control, could see him growing more and more enraged, but it didn't matter. I hated him and I wanted him to be humiliated, to suffer even a little of what we'd had to suffer for the past five years."

"Let's sit down and we can—"

"No. I can't sit." She felt Jack's steady gaze on her as she walked around and around the table, but she couldn't keep still. She had to keep moving. "His friends left and I knew I was going to catch hell, but I was so cocky, I didn't care. When Glenn came into my room, when he slapped me, I didn't even flinch."

"Did you fight back?"

"I wanted to. I wanted to rip him apart. But I learned early on that fighting only made it worse. So I stood there and took it. He hit me and swore at me and called me names, and I took it. Then I told him to go to hell."

When she went by him this time, Jack reached out and stopped her with a hand to her arm. "You stood up to him. That was very brave."

She snorted. "I was an idiot. The words had no sooner left my mouth when the blows changed. Became harder. Faster. He threw me onto my bed and I thought he would leave. That it was over. But he didn't leave. He straddled me and hit me again and again."

She stopped, remembering even then how angry she'd been. How, through the pain and the taste of blood in her mouth, she'd held on to her anger.

"As he was hitting me," she continued, "he kept up the name-calling. Told me he was going to treat me like the whore I was." Her stomach heaved and she inhaled deeply to stop from vomiting. "But it wasn't until he laid on top of me, until I felt his erection as he rubbed against me, that I realized what he meant to do."

And that's when her anger deserted her and the fear set in.

"Is that when Ward came in?"

She shook her head. "He worked for a local carpentry company during the day and took some classes at the community college a few nights a week. Other nights he bussed tables at an Italian restaurant."

"Where was your mother?"

"Tending bar. Glenn had retired from the force and started a security business, but it tanked. Money was tight and Leigh preferred working than being home."

Jack rubbed her arms, his touch soothing. "So it was just you and your stepfather."

She nodded. "When I realized what Glenn was going to do, I went ballistic, punching and kicking him. I must've caught him by surprise because I was able to get past him and into the kitchen. I was almost to the door when he caught me and threw me onto the floor." She could still feel the sharp sting from Glenn pulling her hair, the explosion of pain when he slammed her head against the filthy floor. She could still smell the rankness of his breath as he loomed over her. "He pinned me down with a hand around my neck while he unzipped his pants with the other hand."

She'd clawed at his wrist and arm as panic filled her. But Glenn had just cursed her and tightened his grip. When she'd started crying, he'd banged her head against the floor again. And again. And again until all she'd wanted was to slip into the darkness edging her vision.

"Kelsey?" She looked up into Jack's eyes, saw her own pain reflected there. "You don't have to go on."

"It's okay. I…I want to. I want to tell you."

After a moment, he nodded and settled back against the pool table, pulling her in between his legs. He wrapped his arms around her waist and for the first time that she could remember, she felt safe. Comforted.

"The next thing I knew," she said, "Glenn was sort of lifted off of me. I rolled to my side and saw him and Dillon fighting."

"How did Ward know you were in trouble?"

"He didn't. He'd come home to change before going to the restaurant. Dillon shouted at me to get out, to get help, but…I was so stupid, I couldn't move."

"You weren't stupid," Jack soothed. "You were scared and probably in shock."

"But if I'd gone to get help, if I'd just listened to Dillon in the first place…" God, she'd been such an idiot. "I'd never seen them go at each other before. Glenn was big and a mean drunk. It didn't take long for him to overpower Dillon. He…he kicked Dillon in the head." She remembered the sound of Glenn's foot connecting with Dillon's skull. Her throat clogged, making it difficult to speak. "I thought he was dead."

"You okay?" Jack smoothed her hair back, held her face in his hands as he looked into her eyes. "Do you need a minute?"

She shook her head. If she didn't finish now, she never would. "I couldn't even scream, I just stared at Dillon, willed him to get up, to be okay. When I looked up, Glenn was advancing toward me. His one eye was already swelling shut and his lip was cracked and bloody but he…he had this smile on his face. I got up and grabbed a knife off the counter but my hands were sweaty, and I was shaking so hard, I don't know how I even kept a hold of it. At that moment, I wanted more than anything to kill him."

"I've seen what that type of abuse, that type of terror does to a person," Jack said in his wonderful, calm voice. "How it forces them to do something that under normal circumstances they would never, ever do." He cupped her face in one hand, and her heart broke seeing the pain in his eyes. Pain she knew was for her. "I hate knowing you suffered, that you were forced to endure something that pushed you over the edge that way."

She touched his face, his handsome, strong, decent face and hoped he saw the gratitude she couldn't express. He turned his head and kissed her palm. She curled her fingers and dropped her hand.

"I didn't have the chance to find out how far I'd been

pushed. Glenn lunged at me and twisted my hand back until the bones in my wrist cracked. I dropped the knife.

"Glenn ripped my shirt and yanked my pants down and I knew no one could help me. That Glenn would rape me and my life would never be the same. *I* would never be the same."

"But Dillon stopped him."

"Yes." Thank God. "He had Glenn's softball bat—Glenn had left it by the door. The next thing I knew, there was this…thunk." She swallowed. "Glenn's eyes rolled back and he collapsed. I looked up and saw Dillon swaying on his feet, barely able to stand, still holding the bat."

Jack tipped his head back, blew out a breath. "What I still don't get is how Ward's public defender didn't want to bring this up in court. You were beaten, surely they could've used that to prove Glenn attacked you."

"The cops didn't take my picture—by the time of Dillon's hearing, it was my word against theirs." She gripped his arm. "But you see? He didn't mean to kill Glenn, he was trying to stop him. It wasn't his fault. If I hadn't ditched school or pissed Glenn off—"

"Stop. No more blaming yourself. Ever. Maybe if you hadn't done those things that bastard wouldn't have attacked you—that night. But, he would've another night. And Dillon might not have been around to save you."

He was right. But knowing it didn't make it hurt any less, didn't make her feel any less responsible.

When Jack tugged her toward him, she resisted for all of a second before admitting to herself being held in his arms was exactly where she wanted to be. She slid her arms around his waist and he tucked her head under his chin. The steady rhythm of his heart soothed her.

"Thank you," Jack whispered and placed a soft kiss on the top of her head. "Thank you for telling me. For trusting me."

She did trust him. Completely.

The realization made her jolt back. His brows came together as he looked down at her curiously. Panicked at the emotions churning inside her, at the depths of her feelings, she turned her head and kissed the side of his neck. He stiffened.

"Kelsey," he said gruffly, "I don't think this is what you need now."

Reliving that awful night, telling Jack the truth about what had happened, how it was all her fault, only proved she was no good for someone like him.

Which meant she should break her ties with him. Stop their relationship or whatever it was they had going on before it became even more complicated. Before she lost her heart to him completely. She should end things between them, walk away and not look back.

But not yet. Not tonight.

She forced herself to meet his gaze. To keep her voice steady. "I'm beginning to think you are exactly what I need."

CHAPTER FOURTEEN

JACK'S FINGERS TIGHTENED ON Kelsey's waist. His pulse quickened. She rose up on her toes and gently touched her mouth to his. Though it cost him, he leaned back. "Honey, I don't want to hurt you."

"You won't," she told him solemnly. "You couldn't."

He searched her face. "Maybe I don't want you to hurt me."

She blushed. But instead of pulling away as he expected her to, she said, "I'm no good at making promises, Jack. I don't know what tomorrow's going to bring and I'm scared to death Dillon's going to be arrested for a murder he didn't commit." She lowered her voice to barely a whisper. "That I won't be able to help him. And that he'll never forgive me for letting him down all those years ago."

Her honesty and pain almost undid Jack. He smoothed her hair back. "If Ward is guilty, it isn't your fault."

She covered his hand with her own. "Deep down, I know that. And I don't want you to think this is a replay of the other night, because it's not."

"What is it then?"

"It's...inevitable," she said after a moment. "But tonight I want both of us to go into this with our eyes wide open."

And that's what she did. Kept her eyes open and on his as she edged closer, sliding her hands up his arms and linking them behind his neck. He couldn't stop himself from slipping his fingers under her shirt to touch her warm, soft skin.

Eyes locked on his, Kelsey leaned forward. As their lips met, his head swam. She was so damn hopeful, he thought his racing heart would burst out of his chest. She kissed him again, pressing her mouth to his harder, longer. When her tongue stroked his lips, he groaned in surrender.

She sighed into his mouth and he took the kiss deeper, stroking his hands up her back. He wanted more than anything to strip her bare, to lay her on the pool table and touch and taste every inch of her delectable skin. Feel the tremors of her body under his hands and mouth.

But as much as his body craved the tight feel of hers pulsating around him, he wanted to take his time. He wanted to cherish her.

Reluctantly, he broke the kiss and stood, setting her away from him.

"Jack?" She reached a hand out, clearly disappointed.

He gripped her hand and laid it on his chest. "I was just wondering if that old sleeper sofa I gave Allie is as uncomfortable as I remember."

She smiled, slow and beautiful. "It's not bad," she told him, her voice husky and sexy as hell. "A bit lumpy maybe."

He raised her hand and kissed her knuckles. "I should probably check it out for myself. Just to make sure."

"That's what I like about you, Sheriff. Always practical."

He grinned. They shut off the lights in the bar and walked up the stairs hand in hand. At the top of the stairs, she opened the door to the small apartment and flicked on the overhead kitchen light illuminating the unpainted drywall and newly installed cabinets.

Without a word, she walked down the hallway. As Jack followed her, he had a quick glimpse of a tiny living room filled with boxes and painting supplies, a cramped bathroom and a bedroom in worse shape than the living room.

At the end of the hall, Kelsey turned into a second bedroom. When he reached the room, she'd already turned on a small lamp sitting on an overturned crate. The ugly green sleeper sofa he'd gladly given Allie a few months back was already pulled out, dominating the small room.

It wasn't candlelight and satin sheets, but it would have to do.

He shut the door behind him with a soft click. He stopped next to her and in one smooth move she turned to face him, wrapped her arms around his neck and kissed him. She rubbed against him like a cat, hell, she even sounded like a cat when she purred.

Unable to help himself, he pulled her even closer. When he rolled his hips, she moaned into his mouth, the sound reverberating in his head. He wanted her *now*.

At that thought, he broke the kiss. She frowned and dropped her hands to his chest. "What's wrong now?"

"Nothing." Except that she'd almost made him lose control again. He wanted to take his time and she had him as hot and horny as a teenager. "I thought we'd do something a little… different."

Humor flashed in her eyes. "There are only so many ways to do this, Jack. And all of them have the same end result. Insert tab A into slot B."

"If the end result's the same," he said as he kneaded her

buttocks, "then you won't mind if I take my time getting there."

"Well, now, I guess that depends."

"On?"

"How much time. And what you plan on doing with it."

Despite her smart-ass attitude, she was clearly nervous. He bent his head and kissed her once, a soft lingering kiss. "As much time as it takes until I've had my fill of you. I want my hands on you, Kelsey. All of you. Let me touch you."

KELSEY DIDN'T POINT OUT that he *was* touching her. One of his hands had slipped under her shirt to smooth slow circles over her back while his other hand still cupped her rear. She also didn't mention how, if he hadn't stopped them a moment ago, they'd be on to full-body contact.

He skimmed hot kisses across her jaw and up to her ear. He flicked her earlobe with his tongue before gently biting down. She gasped at the sensation of his teeth against her sensitive flesh.

Jack lifted his head and watched her as he gently caressed her neck with his fingertips. He trailed his fingers up over her chin to her mouth where he outlined her lips with one finger.

"I love your mouth," he whispered before dipping his head for a soft, clinging kiss. "So pretty." Another kiss. "So soft."

He pulled her shirt up and over her head as he reversed their positions so the backs of his legs were against the bed. Dropping the shirt onto the floor, he reached between them and removed her bra. Sitting back on the bed, he pulled her between his legs. Her head fell back as his large hands molded her breasts, his fingers tweaking and gently rolling her nipples.

She watched him from under heavy eyelids. No one had ever looked at her like that before. With desire, yes, but also warmth and sweetness.

Her stomach quivered under his touch as he slipped his fingers down to the waist of her jeans. He unhooked the button, undid the zipper and eased her jeans and panties down her legs.

"Put your hands on my shoulders," he said hoarsely.

She couldn't. Her arms, like her brain, felt heavy and weighted down. She couldn't lift them. Jack solved the problem by bringing them to his shoulders himself before helping her step out of her jeans and panties.

He chuckled. "I've been wondering what this was." He skimmed his finger below her naval, tracing the lines of her dragonfly tattoo and heating her skin. She watched, dazed, as he slid his hand over and brushed a fingertip across her tight curls. Her pelvis contracted.

"You're beautiful," he told her, looking up and meeting her eyes. "You take my breath away."

She quivered under his touch as he smoothed those wonderful, rough hands down her calves and back up behind her legs, pausing to draw circles on the sensitive skin behind her knees. Her breath caught in her throat when he grasped the backs of her thighs and spread her legs. Her knees buckled when he kissed between her thighs.

"Hold on to me," he urged before settling his mouth on her.

Dark pleasure built quickly as his tongue stroked her. She dug her nails into his shoulders, thrust her hips toward him and whimpered in the back of her throat. Heat and longing spiraled through her system and left her panting. She climaxed suddenly, violently, sensation after sensation rolling through her, leaving her body shaking, her muscles weak.

But Jack was there to hold her up. He stood and eased her onto the bed, quickly took off his own clothes and lay down next to her.

She reached out, but he grabbed both of her wrists in his hand. Trapped them above her head. Her fingers curled when he lowered his head and took one beaded nipple into his mouth and sucked. His free hand glided between her thighs. He raised his head and looked into her face as he slowly slid one finger inside her. Then another. She moaned and contracted around him.

She couldn't look away from the intensity, the desire in his eyes as he moved his fingers, stroking her, taking her back to the edge of pleasure. Eyes locked on his, Kelsey felt herself soaring again. A cry ripped from her throat as she came, her hips lifting off the lumpy mattress.

He let go of her hands and leaned away from her. Breathing heavily, she watched through blurry eyes as he covered himself with a condom. She reached for him at the same time he moved over her. Bracketing his weight on his elbows, he pinned her to the mattress, his arousal hard and hot against her stomach.

She held her breath in anticipation, waiting for him to push into her. Instead, he bent his head and kissed her slowly, drugging her senses. His fingertips brushed across her face, her neck and shoulders. The slope of her breasts. She lifted her hips in pure frustration and felt him smile against her lips.

She wanted him *now*.

Damn it, she didn't want sex between them to be sweet. Didn't want him to be considerate and careful and reverent. She wanted, no, she needed him to lose that tight reign he had on his control.

She lifted her head and met his mouth, bit down on his lower lip before running her tongue over it to soothe. Jack groaned and Kelsey pushed his shoulders and clung to him as he rolled onto his back. Straddling him, she bent to kiss him again.

His tongue became more insistent as it tangled with hers, his hands rougher and more demanding as they smoothed over her skin, molded her breasts. She moved up, then slid down on the hard, hot ridge between her legs. He hissed out a breath and grabbed her hips in his hands. Not to stop her, but to move her over him again. And again.

Watching him carefully, she settled her hands on his chest, lifted her hips and took him inside.

The look of completion, of intensity on his face as he stretched her, filled her, was one she'd never forget. The raw emotion in his expression. He grasped her waist and lifted his hips, embedding himself more deeply inside her.

She tipped her head back on a soft moan. She'd meant to push him, to get them both back to the explosive heat of raw sex. But with Jack, she no longer felt so alone.

She rocked her hips, set a slow, easy pace. Soon, sweat beaded on his forehead, his muscles quivered underneath her. With a small smile, Kelsey straightened and placed her hands over his on her waist. She arched her back and increased her pace. His fingers bit into her skin as his body pumped. Harder. Faster. Until she felt herself tumbling yet again. But this time, she didn't go alone. Jack's eyes clouded and a guttural grunt escaped his lips as he followed her over the edge.

She collapsed on top of him. Her skin, like Jack's, was slick with sweat. Her breathing was ragged, her muscles ached, her bones had obviously dissolved, and she couldn't form a coherent thought if her life depended on it.

She giggled. She'd never felt better.

"Under normal circumstances," he murmured against her shoulder, "I might be offended by a woman laughing at this particular time."

She raised her head and grinned down at him. "Your ego's safe. I wasn't laughing at your skills, I'm just—" Realizing what she was about to say, she stopped and tried to slide away, but Jack's arm around her tightened. He pressed her to his side.

"You're just what?" he asked gruffly.

She was happy. And content.

She felt safe and cared for wrapped in his embrace, but that didn't mean she could just blurt out her feelings to him. Especially when she wasn't sure she could trust those feelings. Or herself. "I just feel really good, you know?"

He pressed a kiss to her forehead. "Yeah. I do know." He stroked her arm. "And I'm grateful I don't have to save my reputation by proving how virile I am, seeing as how I can't even move."

"If you want, you could…stay here. Until you've recuperated," she added and then held her breath, waiting.

He stilled. "You sure?"

She nodded. He squeezed her before reaching down and dragging the heavy quilt at the end of the sofa over them. Lying there with her head on Jack's shoulder while he stroked circles over her back, Kelsey exhaled softly.

And hoped like hell she hadn't just done the dumbest thing of all. Fallen in love.

JACK WATCHED KELSEY SLEEP, her breathing deep and even, her lashes dark against the fairness of her face. She was curled up next to him, her hand resting on his chest and one long leg entwined with his. He could get used to waking up next to her.

Which was just the beginning of a whole mess of problems for him.

Unfortunately, he didn't have a choice. They'd connected last night in a way he hadn't thought he'd connect with a woman other than Nicole. In a way he hadn't wanted to connect with another woman. It had started with Kelsey opening up to him about her unrelenting devotion to her brother, and why she felt responsible for Ward being sent to prison.

Thinking about what could have happened to her—what would have happened—if Ward hadn't come along when he did, made Jack's stomach churn. He'd suspected she'd been sexually attacked but he hadn't really wanted to believe it. Now that he knew for certain, he couldn't help but be glad her brother had protected her.

Even though it meant he'd had to take another person's life.

Kelsey snuggled closer to Jack and he slid his hand up her arm. She'd been hurting last night, and she'd needed him to help ease that hurt. But it had turned into so much more.

Maybe he shouldn't have spent the night. He hadn't spent the entire night with a woman since Nicole died. Being involved with her could cost him his job and his reputation. If Ward was guilty of Shannon's murder, Kelsey would have no reason to stay in Serenity Springs. And even less reason to want to be with Jack. Which was probably for the best. After all, Kelsey was sarcastic, often hostile and patently uncomfortable around his daughter.

She was also funny, smart and loyal. Tough enough to survive her childhood, strong enough to overcome it.

Her leg slid higher up his thigh and his body hardened. She was what he wanted. He just needed to convince her that she wanted him as well.

Jack rolled over so that he was on top of her, his weight on his elbows. He kissed her slowly. Even before she fully awoke, she responded to him, returned his kiss, her hips arching up to him.

"Morning," he murmured. She was so damn irresistible, all warm and sleepy.

"Mmm." She smiled before her eyes opened. "Morning." She raised her eyebrows. "Someone woke up happy to see me."

Jack reached over for another condom. "This seems to be becoming a habit."

She linked her hands behind his neck. "You know what they say," she said with a soft smile. "Third time's the charm."

WRAPPED IN A TOWEL, KELSEY looked into the bathroom mirror and tried to contain her satisfied grin as she combed her wet hair. She failed miserably.

The third time hadn't done the trick after all. In an effort to conserve water, she'd joined Jack for a long, steamy shower and a fourth attempt.

Even a diehard morning-hater such as herself would be hard-pressed to stay in bed knowing Jack was waiting for her. What that man could do with just his hands and a bar of soap was amazing. Add in some hot water and his tongue? Incredible.

Humming under her breath, she finger-styled her hair, allowing it to air dry. Sex with Jack was so far beyond anything she'd ever experienced, it might just be worth risking her heart.

She tipped her head to the side and scrunched up her nose at her reflection. Not that she had any choice about it now.

Tightening the towel around her, she headed back to the bedroom to find Jack already dressed.

"I have to stop by the station for a few hours this morning," he told her. "But other than that, I'm off duty." He looked around. Seeing his wallet on the floor, he bent to pick it up and stuck it in his back pocket. "I need to pick Emma up at Nina's at eleven."

"Well, you'd better go then," she said, telling herself it was dumb to feel disappointed. He had a life. A career and a child that needed his attention.

"I guess I'd better." Except he didn't go anywhere. "I'll see you later?" He made it sound like a question.

Her heart about stopped. Was he asking if he could see her later? Did he want to see her later?

She had no clue how to proceed, what to say. "If you want," she said, leaving the decision up to him.

He frowned and walked up to her. "You could come over."

She blinked. "Huh?"

"When I'm done with work. You could come to the house and spend the day with me."

"What about Emma?"

"Emma, too. It's nothing exciting, we were just going to hang out, maybe rent a couple videos."

"You…you want me to spend the day with you and your daughter?"

"I do."

She recognized the warm, bright feeling as hope and ramped down on it ruthlessly.

"You don't need to worry about me." Because it hurt to look at him, she turned and began rummaging through her duffel bag for clean clothes. "Just because I told you…what I told you…" She had to stop, clear her throat. "I'm okay. You don't have to babysit me."

"Is that what you think I'm doing?"

She shuffled to the other side of the sofa bed. "I'm not sure," she said truthfully.

He tipped his head back, blew out a breath. "I want to spend time with you." As if he knew she was powerless against it, he smiled at her. "Come on, it could be fun. Emma would love to see you."

"I thought we were going to keep this—" she gestured to the bed "—between us. No kid involved."

He scratched his head. "That was the plan, but…"

"But?"

"Plans change. And I thought maybe we could see where things go. Between you and me."

"You want to see where things go?"

"Yeah. I do."

Her heart lodged in her throat. The idea of spending time with Jack and Emma was too appealing to pass up. "I could stop by for a little while," she finally said.

He grinned. "Great. Why don't you come over for lunch?"

"I have some things to do here… I'm not sure how long it's going to take."

"Fine." He settled his mouth on hers for a tender, lingering kiss that curled her toes. "I'll see you soon."

After Jack walked out the door, Kelsey fell back onto the sofa and wondered what in the hell she'd gotten herself into now.

CHAPTER FIFTEEN

JACK CLOSED HIS OFFICE DOOR behind Officer Andrew Flick. Dark, hard looks, and a build like the linebacker he'd been both in high school and college made Flick an imposing presence. Yet underneath the physique was a keen mind and good instincts.

He liked Flick, but more importantly, he trusted him. Which was why he'd assigned Flick the job of staking out the area around the Crandall's house. People were incredibly predictable in their habits, rarely veering off their daily routine. For the past week, Flick had surveyed Edgewood Lane, but nothing out of the ordinary had come up. Until last night.

Jack motioned for the other man to sit in one of the chairs facing his desk. "Tell me about the Douglass kid," Jack said as he sat behind his desk.

"He arrived around twelve-fifteen. At first, I thought he was just turning around. But then he backed into a small clearing and shut off his lights."

"He didn't see you?"

"I'd kept my car hidden."

Jack picked up Flick's report and skimmed it. "You approached Douglass's car?"

"I did. He sat there waiting for a good ten minutes before I approached him." Flick flashed a quick grin. "Scared the crap out of him when I knocked on his window."

"I bet."

"When I asked him if there was a problem, he started stammering on about how he was having car trouble, that he just dropped his girlfriend off and he stalled out."

"You stated in your report he seemed nervous."

"Could barely meet my eyes. Kept looking down the road toward the houses."

"Think he was staking out the houses to rob?" Last month, a couple of teenagers had been picked up for robberies, but they mostly stuck to the homes of people they knew, robbing them during the day while they were at work.

"I don't think so. He was nervous, but cocky, too. When I pointed out that I saw him pull into this spot from the opposite direction he claimed, he changed tactics. Tried telling me that he meant he'd forgotten something at his girlfriend's house. He was going back to get it but since the lights were off, he changed his mind."

"Did he say who the girlfriend is?"

"Amy Schuman. When I asked him to try the engine, it started right up. "

"You think he was meeting his girlfriend?"

"Possible. Although she never showed up."

"He could've contacted her after he left."

"Yep. You think this is usual, them sneaking out together?"

"Could be. Only way we're going to find out is to talk to both of them."

"I didn't see them at any other time during the past week."

"School nights might play a part in that," Jack said. "And isn't Douglass on the football team?"

"He's their top running back."

"Which means he was out of town Friday night."

Flick stood. "You want me to call both kids in?"

"No. Let's go to them. Maybe they'll be more cooperative that way."

Flick left and Jack sat back. If Amy Schuman had planned on sneaking out with her boyfriend last night, then it was possible she'd snuck out last Saturday night, too.

He had to know for sure. Hell, it was a long shot, but one he needed to take. He was running out of time.

And if Amy had been out last Saturday night—and not sleeping in her bed as she'd claimed when she was questioned after the murder—then she might have seen something. Something that could possibly help Jack with this investigation. Or at least point him in the right direction.

He just hoped, for Kelsey's sake, that if Amy did have any new information, it didn't point to Dillon Ward.

"WHAT DO YOU WANT NOW?" Dillon asked.

Kelsey refused to let his hostility affect her. She'd been on her way to Jack's, nervous and excited about spending a few hours with Jack and Emma when she'd found herself pulled over in front of Dillon's apartment.

"For starters," she said as she shivered in the cold wind, "I'd like to come in."

This time, she waited to be invited inside. Which he did, albeit reluctantly. She walked inside, the aroma of baked goods from below permeating the air.

"I was on my way over to The Summit," he said as he sat and pulled on a pair of shiny new work boots. She guessed the police hadn't returned his other pair after taking them in as possible evidence.

"This won't take long."

He glanced up at her. "The last time you said that, I got arrested."

"You weren't arrested. You were taken in for questioning." She shook her head. "But that's not why I'm here. For the past week you've managed to drown me out or ignore me or get rid of me, but not this time."

He tied his laces and stood, towering over her. "Looks like your temper hasn't mellowed any."

"That's what I'm talking about. I've been trying to show you, to prove to you that I've grown up and changed, but you won't accept it."

"People don't change."

"You have. You're doing exactly what you always warned me about. You let your hostility and anger control you. God, you used to be someone I could look up to, someone who fought for what they believed in."

"I fought, yeah, but I played by the rules," he argued. "I watched while that bastard hurt you and Leigh. I waited for the right people to take care of it. I trusted in the system and what did it get me? Or you? You were attacked. Glenn would've raped you. And then he probably would've killed you."

"But he didn't. You saved me." She wanted to reach out to him, but the look on his face said her touch wouldn't be welcome. Her tears spilled over. "I'm sorry it took so long for me to realize what you'd been trying to teach me all those years."

"What are you talking about?"

"The way you used to take care of me, how you wanted me to be a better person, to toe the line." She forced herself to maintain eye contact. "I was so angry all the time, I thought you wanted me to be good to make your life easier."

Dillon stabbed his hand through his hair. "What's this all about, Kelsey?"

"I'm done. I'm done chasing you."

"Giving up? Doesn't sound like you've changed much after all."

"I'm not giving up," she told him fiercely, wiping away her tears. "I'll never give up on you. But I am done trying to force you into a relationship you don't want. If you need me, I'll be here."

"Here? In Serenity Springs?" He narrowed his eyes. "Why?"

An image of Jack looking up at her as they'd made love last night filled her brain. She sniffed and avoided Dillon's eyes. "I've decided to stick around for a while. Allie needs help at the bar—"

"You're not staying to help Allie. You're staying for Martin."

"Does it matter? Either way, I'm not going anywhere."

"Because you want to save me? To make things how they used to be between us? Or because you want Jack Martin?"

She swallowed. "I never said Jack and I—"

"It's all over town. Everyone knows the chief's sleeping with the prime murder suspect's sister."

Her blood froze. "It's not like that."

Dillon cut his hand viciously through the air as if to wipe away her words. "Doesn't matter what it's really like. Haven't you learned that by now? You need to watch yourself."

"Maybe I'm tired of keeping to myself," she burst out. "Tired of pushing people away. Of being alone."

"That's the only way. Yeah, you've changed, but so what? It's not enough. It'll never be enough. You'll never fit in with these people. You can't. Call it genetics, circumstances—" He shook his head in disgust. "Call it whatever the hell you want. People like us, we can't trust someone enough to love them the way they deserve to be loved."

"You're wrong," she whispered, but his words shook her to the core.

"Am I?" he asked with such resignation that Kelsey's heart broke. For both of them.

"I know what you gave up for me, what saving me cost you," she said softly. "I want you to know I'll never forgive myself for what happened." He backed away from her, his expression stony.

That's when she realized what Jack had been telling her was true. Her brother had changed. The boy she'd looked up to, the young man who'd been her hero was long gone.

"You always told me all the trouble I caused would come back to bite me in the ass. But it didn't. It came back and bit you instead, and for that I'm sorry—" She shut her mouth when her voice broke. "So sorry."

"I don't blame you," Dillon said in exasperation. "I never did."

"Then why did you send me away? Why didn't you want me to visit you in prison?"

"You think I wanted my little sister seeing me locked up like a goddamn animal?" He stopped, his mouth a grim line. "I didn't want you to see me that way. I had to change, to become a different man, to survive."

"So you sent me away. To protect me?"

He smiled sadly. "It's a tough habit to break. But that

wasn't the only reason. I'm not a saint, Kelsey. Even though what happened wasn't your fault, I was still angry."

She nodded. "At me."

"You. Glenn. Myself. If I'd had more control that night, if I'd gotten you out of the house before he could—"

"None of that was your fault." She remembered Jack telling her the same thing the night before. "Glenn was sick. Evil. And I'm sorry for what happened. For what you had to do."

"I regret a lot of things," he said, "but I've never regretted stopping Glenn from hurting you. Never."

"Thank you," she said huskily. "I'd better let you get going." She didn't want to push this tenuous truce. Didn't want to push her luck too far.

She crossed to the door. Her hand was on the knob when his voice stopped her. "Are you really staying in Serenity Springs?"

"Yes," she said, convinced she'd made the right choice. "I really am. Maybe we could do this again? Talk, I mean?"

"Maybe," he conceded. "Just…do me a favor?"

"Anything."

"This thing with you and Jack Martin—"

"I told you—"

"Yeah, I know what you told me. Just…promise me you'll be careful."

WITH THE PHONE AT HIS EAR, Jack looked out the window again, but saw no sign of Kelsey's car. He turned and waited for Seth to pick up the phone. Though he hadn't talked to his best friend since they met at The Summit last week, he knew he could count on Seth to help him out.

"Hello?"

"Where the hell have you been?" Jack asked, walking into the hallway where the Disney movie Emma was watching couldn't be heard. "Didn't you get my messages?"

"Mom? Is that you?"

"Funny. Listen, I need your help."

"What's up?"

"I've had a break in the Crandall case." He paced the floor. "I need you to check some phone records for me."

"Why can't you check them yourself?"

"I don't want anyone in the department to know about this." He crossed to the window again. "I found out the Schumans' fifteen-year-old daughter has been sneaking out in the middle of the night to meet her boyfriend. She was out last Friday night and saw a car parked at Shannon's."

Seth whistled. "What do you want run?"

Jack wiped a hand over his face and recited the numbers he wanted traced. "Get back to me as soon as you get the information."

"Sure thing."

He hung up and put the phone back on the small table in the hallway.

"Wanna play a game with me, Daddy?" Emma asked when he walked back into the living room.

"Sure. Why don't you run upstairs and bring one down?"

She raced upstairs and Jack glanced out the window to see Kelsey pulling into the driveway. He wasn't sure if the new information Amy provided would help him solve Shannon's murder or not. Hell, it wasn't much to go on, but he hoped the phone records would provide more insight.

Though he had a few more clues, a few more pieces to the puzzle, he still had nothing concrete. Certainly nothing that would justify making an arrest. Only a gut feeling that he was getting close to discovering who the guilty party was. And that it wasn't Dillon Ward.

But was he having that feeling because of his instincts, or because he wanted Kelsey's brother to be innocent?

The doorbell rang. He opened the door and immediately noticed Kelsey's nervousness. She clutched the strap of her purse on her shoulder, her knuckles white.

Unbelievably pleased to see her, he grinned and stepped back to let her in. "Hey."

"Hi."

"Kelsey!" Emma cried from the top of the stairs. "What are you doing here?"

Kelsey, in the act of taking off her coat, met Jack's eyes. "You didn't tell her I was coming over?"

"And have her ask me every five minutes when you were getting here?" He took her coat and purse and hung them in the hall closet. "No."

Emma scurried down the stairs. She skidded to a stop in front of them and wrapped her arms around Kelsey's knees.

Kelsey patted her head. "Hey, kid. I thought I'd stop by, see what you and your dad were up to."

"We're going to play a game," Emma said, already dragging Kelsey farther inside the house by the hand. "You can play, too."

They went into the living room where Emma led Kelsey over to the cold fireplace. "You stand here. Don't move. I'll go up and get the game and be right back." She looked at Kelsey. "Do you want to play Candy Land or Memory?"

Jack turned his back so Emma wouldn't see his lips moving. "Memory," he whispered beneath his breath. "If you don't want to spend the entire afternoon stuck in Molasses Swamp, then for the love of God, pick Memory."

Kelsey laughed.

"What's so funny?" Emma wanted to know.

"Uh, nothing," Kelsey said. "I, uh, I'm just so happy you want to play Memory. It's one of my favorites."

"Thank you," Jack said after Emma had climbed the stairs. "Trying to draw a double orange card is its own kind of hell."

"I'll take your word for it."

Their eyes locked and their smiles slipped away. Kelsey broke the spell by looking away.

"You have a nice house. I mean, I know I've been in it before, but I wasn't in it, just the kitchen and the…uh…" Her face flushed and he wondered if, like him, she was thinking of the laundry room. "I mean, not in this room—"

"Thanks," he said, taking pity on her. "We like it."

She nodded, turned suddenly and knocked over one of the framed photos on the mantel. "Sorry." Since her hands seemed none too steady, he helped her right the picture. "Is this your wife?"

He glanced down at the framed photo of a smiling Nicole and nodded.

"She was very pretty."

"Yeah. She was." He ran a finger down the front of the frame and realized that while he had no problem admitting he found his deceased wife pretty, he'd never gotten around to telling Kelsey the same thing. At least not when they were fully clothed.

"You're pretty," he said. She raised her eyebrows. "I mean…you look pretty today. In that outfit."

Now she frowned. Glanced down at her jeans and gray sweatshirt. "You don't have to say that, Jack. They're just words. Words I don't need—"

Her voice dropped off when he cupped her cheek in his hand. Her eyes widened.

"Even though you might not need them, I want to say them." He stepped closer until their bodies brushed. He lowered his voice. "I think you're beautiful."

Because she still didn't look like she believed him, he decided to prove it to her. He bent down and gently kissed her, his eyes drifting shut, his heart stumbling in his chest at the contact.

He kept the kiss soft. Tender. Loving.

Jack lifted his head and forced his eyes open, saw his own confusion mirrored in the green depths of her eyes. He cleared his throat. "Kelsey, I—"

"I got Memory."

Emma stood in the doorway, the card game in her hand, a huge grin splitting her face.

"Great." Jack stepped back, shoved his hands in his pockets and told himself it was for the best. Until he knew for certain her brother was innocent, until he could prove it, what he felt for Kelsey, what he'd been about to say to her, was better left unsaid.

THE KID WAS SOME SORT OF WEIRD cardsharp. They'd played Memory five times and Emma had won all but the last game. Kelsey wasn't sure how she felt about a six-year-old having better short-term recollection than her.

"Are you still pouting?" Jack asked as he rinsed a plate under the hot water.

"I'm not pouting." She took the plate from him and began to dry it. "I'm just curious how you knew where that last match was, when you spent most of your time making phone calls."

And she was curious what all those phone calls were about. Not that Jack seemed interested in sharing.

"I have my ways," he said with a grin.

She snorted. It was his fault her concentration had been off, anyway. All she'd been able to think about was that amazingly sweet kiss he'd laid on her. Her heart still hadn't recovered.

"Kelsey, I made this for you." Emma held up a drawing. "It's you, me and Daddy."

Kelsey dried off her hands and took the paper. A lump formed in her throat to see three stick figures—one with a halo of yellow hair, one orange hair and a tall one with black hair. Every stick figure had a huge smile on their face, and to complete the picture, Emma had written her name and the word *love* across the bottom in careful letters.

"Do you like it?" Emma asked. "I worked real hardly on it."

"It's great," she said, her voice husky. "Thanks."

"You can hang it on your 'frigerator.'"

"I will," she promised, thinking of the minifridge in the kitchen above The Summit. "As soon as I get home."

Of course she'd have to stop at the store and buy a magnet first, but it would be worth it.

"Do you like it, Daddy?"

Kelsey forced herself to look up at Jack. He was staring back at her, his expression unreadable. "It's terrific, squirt. A masterpiece." While Emma beamed, Jack glanced at his watch. "Bath time, kiddo."

The phone rang. "I got it," Emma sang out. She picked it up, said hello, listened a moment and then held it out. "It's for you, Daddy."

He took the phone but instead of speaking into it, he covered the mouthpiece with his hand. "This might take a while," he told Kelsey. "Could you help Emma get ready for bed?"

"I don't know how," she blurted.

Humor lit his eyes. "She's old enough to do most of it herself. I just need you to keep an eye on her while she takes a bath and make sure she brushes her teeth."

Kelsey was all set to make up some excuse about how she had to get home and wash her hair, but Emma grabbed a hold of her hands and hopped up and down.

"We'll have a lot of fun," Emma said excitedly. "And I'll be really good. I promise."

Oh, man. "Uh, I guess I could help her."

"I appreciate it," Jack said. "I'll come up as soon as I'm done."

"Yay!" Emma pulled her out of the room. "Come on."

"I'll be up to kiss you good-night in a little bit," Jack called after them.

As Kelsey stumbled up the stairs behind a chattering Emma she couldn't help but hope he was talking to her as well as his daughter.

JACK WAITED UNTIL EMMA and Kelsey had disappeared up the stairs before speaking into the phone. "What did you find?"

"The number you gave me had four incoming calls last Friday night," Seth said. "Sorry, buddy. None were from Shannon Crandall."

With his free hand Jack pinched the bridge of his nose. He'd been so sure this hunch would pan out. "Did you trace all the calls?"

"Three were from his mother, which almost makes me feel sorry for the poor sap. The last one was from a cell phone, but the name and number aren't local."

"Who was it?"

"Tess Rennard from Tampa Bay."

Adrenaline zipped through his veins. "That's our connection."

"What is?"

"Tess Rennard is Shannon's sister." He grabbed Shannon's file off the counter and searched through the papers until he found Tess's personal information. "What's the cell's number?"

Seth recited the digits. "He received the call at 12:13 a.m."

Jack scanned the paper listing Tess's address, e-mail address, home, work and cell numbers. "It doesn't match the information I have, but the timing's right." He tapped the paper twice. "I need to get hold of Tess. See what she knows. Thanks for the help."

"No problem. Let me know if you need anything else."

Frowning, Jack hung up the phone. If his instincts were right, Serenity Springs was about to have one hell of a scandal on its hands.

His brain went into cop mode. Now wasn't the time for speculation. What he needed were facts. The phone call from Tess was a connection but it didn't prove anything.

It was up to him to find that proof.

He picked up the phone and dialed Tess's home number. "Ms. Rennard," he said when she picked up. "It's Chief Jack Martin. I have a few questions I need to ask you."

CHAPTER SIXTEEN

KELSEY STOOD IN FRONT OF Emma's closet and held up a bright-blue sweater. "How about this one?"

Emma sat on her bed. Her forehead wrinkled. "No. I wore that the other day."

Kelsey tamped down her impatience and reached into the closet. Honestly, the kid was picky. Jeez, just throw something on. You're six years old. Who cares what you look like?

Emma had emerged from her bath slightly wrinkled, flushed pink, and—this was the important part—clean. She'd brushed her teeth without being reminded and had allowed Kelsey to pull a comb through her soft, damp hair.

Then came story time. While having Emma curl up against her as they'd sat together on the bed had been okay, enough was enough already. Where was Jack?

Kelsey pulled out the next shirt without even looking at it. "How about—"

"Yes. That one." Emma bounced on her knees. "I want to wear that one. Yellow is Brian's favorite color."

Thank you, God. And thank you, Brian, whoever you are. "Great. Yellow it is."

"Brian is my boyfriend," Emma said as she slid under her covers. "We're going to get married."

Kelsey raised her eyebrows. Laid the shirt with the socks, jeans and shoes that were on Emma's dresser. "Aren't you a little young?"

"We're not going to get married now." Her *duh* may have been silent, but it was definitely implied. "When we're growned ups."

"Ah, well, drop me a line, maybe I'll come to the wedding."

"You can be in it if you want and I can be the flower girl when you and daddy get married."

The air rushed out of Kelsey's lungs. She tried to draw in a breath but her chest was too tight. "Jack and I aren't getting married."

"You have to marry daddy so you can be my mommy."

Mommy.

Oh my God.

Kelsey's knees gave out and she slid down to the edge of the bed. "I don't know what's given you the idea that your dad and I...that we're going to—"

"I saw you kissing."

Her heart drummed heavily in her chest. That kiss had been...well, she wasn't sure what it had been. But it sure hadn't been a marriage proposal.

"Uh, you know, just because I kissed Jack—your dad— doesn't mean... It isn't... He was helping me get something out of my eye."

"No he wasn't. He kissed you. I saw it."

"So we kissed. It's no big deal. Sometimes men and women...grown-up men and women... What I mean is..." She was so not getting into a discussion about the birds and the bees with this kid. "Look, sometimes a kiss is just a kiss."

Emma blinked innocently. "When you marry Daddy, you can live with us and you could be my mommy and then you could get me a baby brother."

Oh. My. God.

Emma, obviously unaware Kelsey was having a freaking heart attack, kept talking. "You could live with us and sleep with Daddy. Hayley said when her mommy and daddy lived together they slept in the same bed and that's how babies are made."

That Hayley kid was chock-full of information, wasn't she?

"Can we name my baby brother Bob?" Emma asked.

"Hey, whoa, slow down a minute." Kelsey tried to swallow but her mouth was too damn dry. "I'm not going to marry Jack and I'm not going to be anybody's mommy."

She would never do that to a poor kid. She'd make a terrible mother.

What Emma needed was another mother like the one the girl had had. Someone sweet. Someone Jack could fall in love with, someone he wanted to spend his life with. Someone he was proud to share his life with.

Not someone like her.

"You don't like me," Emma said, her lower lip quivering, her big eyes filled with tears.

Don't cry. Please don't cry. "I didn't say that." Okay, that sounded harsh. She worked on gentling her tone. "Of course I like you."

"Really?"

Kelsey nodded, surprised and scared to realize it was true. She did like Emma. But that didn't mean she wanted to keep her.

"Really. But you don't want me as your...to be your mother." She forced back the sense of panic creeping up her spine. "I'd make a terrible mother. I have hair like a boy, remember? You don't want a mommy who looks like a boy, do you?"

Emma tilted her head, her eyes miraculously tear-free. "I like your hair."

She gritted her teeth. "I can't cook, I hate to clean and I don't like to do other people's laundry."

"You don't have to. Daddy has Mrs. Crawley come in and clean and sometimes she washes clothes, too."

"I don't know anything about kids." That much was true. The only thing she knew about kids was that they were small, smelled funny and needed a lot of attention. "I don't have enough patience to be a mother. I don't know any fairy tales or kid songs."

Emma sighed as she snuggled under her covers. "That's okay. I can teach you some songs and you can help me make cookies."

The kid was totally missing the point. "I only know how to make one type of cookie, and...and I'd make you eat your vegetables. And clean your own room. And take out the garbage."

"That's what all moms do." Emma yawned. "And kids are supposed to eat vegetables. They're good for us."

The kid had it all figured out. "I'm sorry but I just can't be your mommy."

Emma peered up at her through heavy-lidded eyes and smiled. "Yes, you will," she said with such conviction, Kelsey's heart jumped. "Now you kiss me good-night," Emma said, reaching out.

Kelsey leaned over and kissed Emma's puckered lips. Before she could straighten, Emma wrapped her arms around her neck and held on tight.

Tears sprang to her eyes. She blinked them back and, as gently as she could, untangled herself from Emma's grip.

"Good night, Kelsey. Could you send Daddy up now?"

Unable to force words past the lump in her throat, she nodded. In the hallway, she quietly shut Emma's door, leaned back against it and closed her eyes.

What was she going to do? Things were getting way out of control. She rubbed a hand over her racing heart. First thing she needed to do was tell Jack. He'd talk to Emma.

They were having a fling. The idea of them together forever, raising Emma, maybe having a few kids of their own, was ridiculous. Even if she could easily picture them all being together. Being a family.

Not. She'd end up hurting the people she'd come to love.

Love. She thumped the back of her head against the door. Oh, God. She couldn't love Jack and Emma. She wouldn't.

She knew what she had to do. Kelsey opened her eyes and pushed away from the door. At the top of the stairs she heard a sharp knock on the front door followed by Jack's low greeting. Unsure whether or not to interrupt, she paused midway down the stairs.

A feminine voice told Jack, "I'm sorry, but my hands are tied. If you don't arrest Dillon Ward tonight, you'll be out of a job and could very well lose your badge."

JACK KEPT HIS VOICE SOFT, hoping Mayor Michaels would follow suit. "This investigation is ongoing—"

"The council doesn't want to hear that," the mayor said. She sighed. "You should have arrested Ward right after the murder."

"I have a new lead. I can promise you there will be an arrest soon."

For a moment, the mayor seemed taken aback. "It's too late. Mark Crandall has already called an emergency meeting of city council for tomorrow morning at 8:00 a.m. You need to be there."

"Jack's doing all he can to find this murderer," Kelsey said hotly as she descended the stairs and stood next to him. "Who the hell are you to be talking to him this way?"

"This is Christine Michaels. The *mayor*."

Christine blushed, her eyes flashing. She turned her back on Kelsey. "She's here? In your house? Do you think that's wise when everyone in town already thinks you're sleeping with her?"

"I have nothing to hide, and let's keep our voices down. My daughter is asleep upstairs."

"You should have thought of your daughter before you got involved with her." The mayor sniffed. "Your relationship with her and your refusal to arrest Mr. Ward is the reason your job is on the line."

He gritted his teeth. "I haven't done anything immoral or illegal."

"Besides your…relationship with this…woman being unacceptable, you stood up for her instead of one of the officers under your supervision." The mayor pointed at Kelsey. "She threatened Ben while you stood by. I know all about it, just as I know you have no intention of arresting her brother so you can continue keeping this woman in your bed."

Jack stepped forward, narrowing his eyes. "Don't overstep."

Mayor Michaels drew herself up. "It's you who've overstepped. And to think, I defended you to city council. Well, no more. Once the council members hear how you endangered the life of a subordinate, and how your mistake in New York got a man killed, it's you who'll pay the price."

She whirled and stormed out, slamming the door behind her. Enraged, Jack clenched and unclenched his hands. He tipped his head back, breathing heavily, before looking at Kelsey.

Her arms were crossed, she was chewing her lower lip. He saw worry. And guilt.

"What's going on?" he asked.

"What do you mean?"

"I mean, I'm surprised you didn't rip the mayor's head off. Not that I don't appreciate your restraint, but—"

"This is all my fault."

He reached for her. "No, it's—"

"It is." She moved away from him and he let his hands fall to his sides. Kelsey crossed to the door. "If you weren't involved with me, you could do your job and no one would question your decisions. Your motives. Damn it, Jack. They're going to fire you because of me."

"I'm not going to lose my job," he assured her.

"How can you say that? Didn't you hear what she said? City council's out for blood. *Your* blood. And thanks to the mayor finding me here, you've lost an ally."

He thought of telling her about his new lead, but something held him back. "Trust me," he said as he reached out and stroked her cheek. "My job is safe."

She pulled away from him. "I don't think we should see each other anymore."

He went very still.

She attempted to go around him but he grabbed her by the arm. "What's the deal, Kelsey?"

"Look, it's been fun," she said with a shrug, "but things are getting too complicated for me. You investigating Dillon, this whole thing with the mayor and city council, and now Emma…" She pressed her lips together.

"What about Emma?"

"She saw us kissing in the living room. Now she's got some crazy idea in her head that you and I are getting married."

The panic in her voice made him feel queasy. "And you don't want that."

She averted her gaze. "It's just better for everyone if we end things now."

"That's it?" He fought to keep his temper in check. "One innocent comment and you decide, hey, it's been nice, but we're through?" He shook his head. "I don't think so. Because I'm not done with you. Not by a long shot."

"You wanted to see where things went between us, and now we've gone as far as we can go. It's no big deal. We're two unattached adults who had sex—"

"Bullshit." The curse, said quietly, was heated. Damn it, he wasn't going to let her push him away. "Last night was a hell of a lot more than us screwing each other."

She flinched, her face losing color but when she spoke, it was with a sneer. "Get over yourself. We had great sex. But that's all it was."

"And now you want it to end?"

"Yes."

The phone rang but Jack ignored it. "What if I don't?"

Her startled gaze shot to his and she stumbled back a step. "Wha…what?"

Another ring. "What if I don't want it to end?"

To his shock, she teared up. "Jack...don't. It's no use."

When the phone rang a third time, Jack cursed inwardly. "I'm sorry," he said. "But I have to take this."

Kelsey nodded once, relief flicking across her face before she looked out the dark window.

Jack stalked to the phone. "Martin," he barked into the receiver.

"We've got it," Flick said without preamble.

"I'll be there in five minutes." He hung up and turned to Kelsey. "I have to go. Can you stay with Emma until I get back?"

She stared at him incredulously, her eyes red rimmed. "You're leaving? Now?"

"I have to," he said simply, though there was nothing simple about the situation. "Something's come up."

She stepped forward. "About Shannon's case? What is it?"

"I can't get into it right now, Kelsey. You're going to have to trust me."

"I'm not sure I can."

Her answer was like a shot to the heart. "I'm trusting you."

"To babysit for you."

"I'm trusting you to watch my child while I go to work." He searched her face. "And I'm trusting you to be here when I get back. Doesn't that mean anything to you?"

"It does," she admitted after a moment. "But I'm not sure I want it to."

Damn it. He didn't have time to get into this now. And while he'd like to believe she'd simply been spooked by Emma and the mayor, that she didn't want to end things between them any more than he did, he couldn't be certain. "Allie's number is by the phone. If you don't want to stay, call her and explain I had an emergency. She'll come over."

Kelsey didn't say anything, but the look in her eyes said she was ready to run. With his heart on the line, he strode over to her and gave her a brief, hard kiss.

"I hope you don't call her," he said, his voice husky with emotion. "I hope you're still here when I get home."

But as he walked out into the cold, he couldn't help but wonder if that wasn't the last he'd ever see of Kelsey Reagan.

KELSEY PICKED UP THE PHONE only to slam it down again. She pulled both hands through her hair and tugged. During the hour Jack had been gone, she'd checked on Emma twice, picked up the phone at least a dozen times—without ever making a call—and worried endlessly about why Jack had rushed off in the first place.

Had he gone to arrest Dillon?

She'd told Jack she could handle whatever happened, but the truth was, she couldn't bear to see her brother arrested. In her heart, she couldn't believe Dillon was capable of murder.

And she couldn't sit back and watch while Jack lost his job and reputation because of her. God. She'd messed up royally. Both Dillon and Jack would be better off without her.

Which was why she needed to call Allie and tell her to come over. Then Kelsey would be free and clear to take off. She could be back in New York before morning. Back to her cramped apartment, her secondhand furniture and her dead-end job.

The thought left a sour taste in her mouth. She paced the

length of the short hallway. Besides, she didn't *have* a dead-end job anymore. Damn it, she didn't want to go back to New York.

She slammed to a halt. Her palms grew clammy and the air backed up in her lungs. She struggled to breathe normally. Of course she wanted to go back. She loved the city. The excitement. The variety. The…the…

Her mind blanked. Oh, man. She was so screwed. Because she really didn't want to go back to her lonely, solitary existence. What she wanted was right here in Serenity Springs.

A job at The Summit where she was appreciated and respected. An employer who wasn't just her boss, but also a friend. A chance to get reacquainted with her brother, to make amends. She wanted to hang out with Emma, to play games with her and listen to her nonstop chatter.

And she wanted Jack. More than she'd ever thought possible.

She shook her head. She couldn't stay. No matter how much it hurt, she had to do what was right. She couldn't afford to be impulsive or reckless. Not this time. There was too much at stake.

She took a deep, shaky breath and wiped her damp palms down the back of her jeans. Before she changed her mind, she dialed and waited impatiently for Allie to pick up. The floor creaked behind her and she turned, expecting to find Emma, but the hall and stairway were both empty.

"Hello?" Allie said.

Trying to shake off the creepy feeling that she was being watched, she said, "It's Kelsey. Jack wanted me to see if you could come to his house and sit with Emma for a while."

"Why didn't Jack call?"

Kelsey shifted the phone to her other ear. "He had to take off suddenly."

"Where are you?"

"I'm here." She rolled her eyes because obviously Allie didn't know where "here" was. "I'm at Jack's. But I need to leave."

"I'll be right over," Allie promised before disconnecting.

The dial tone buzzed in Kelsey's ear and she tightened her grip on the phone. Shortly, she'd be out of Jack's life forever.

The floor creaked again and this time, the nape of Kelsey's neck prickled. Before her vague sense of unease could become full-fledged panic, pain exploded in the back of her head. She crumpled to the floor as blackness engulfed her.

JACK WALKED INTO HIS OFFICE and picked up Shannon Crandall's file. After Flick phoned Jack at home to let him know they had the warrants to search the Michaels' house and barn, they'd gathered enough evidence to bring Ben Michaels in for Shannon's murder. The D.A. was ready to press charges tonight. But Jack wasn't so sure.

He sat on the edge of his desk and began to go through the papers. They'd brought Ben in for questioning and Jack had laid out the evidence against him: the mud found on Shannon's floor had horse grain in it—most likely from the Michaels's barn, an eyewitness saw Ben's cruiser at the Crandall residence three hours before Mark Crandall called 911. They had phone records that showed Ben received a call on his cell phone from an account set up in Tess Rennard's name, an account Tess admitted Shannon set up so she could contact her lover without her husband finding out.

Cornered, Ben had admitted that he and Shannon were

involved until she'd ended things a few weeks ago. That, the night she died, she'd called him and he'd gone to her house. He admitted they had sex but claimed he hadn't killed her. He'd broken down then, had sobbed that he'd loved her and could never hurt her. He'd wanted her to leave her husband. When Shannon refused, when she gave him the cell phone and told Ben she didn't need it, or him, any longer, Ben claimed he'd been heartbroken. But not angry.

And he swore that when he left, she was still alive.

They'd found the cell phone tucked under Ben's mattress. They'd also discovered that the night of Shannon's murder, one of the Michaels's horses was sick with colic and had needed to be checked on several times during the night. There was a clear view from the front of the Michaels's barn to the Crandall house. It would've been easy enough for Ben to see Ward's truck, to know that the woman he loved was with another man.

They'd taken three pairs of tall rubber boots to the lab to be tested for evidence, along with a twitch—a tool used to restrain horses. It had a chain loop at the end of an eighteen-inch long wooden handle. A handle that was covered with dark specks that looked suspiciously like blood.

Jack found the police log from that night. He scanned it quickly and shook his head. Ben and the other officer on duty that night had responded to a domestic disturbance at 2:10 a.m. and had brought the husband in on an unrelated outstanding warrant. By the time Ben had processed the guy, it was close to three.

Phone records indicate Mark Crandall spoke to his wife at 1:38 a.m.

Either Michaels went back to the Crandall residence

between 3:00 and 3:30 a.m.—when her body was discovered—or someone else killed her.

Perhaps someone close to Ben? Suddenly Jack was on his feet. Holy God. What if Ben was telling the truth?

The door burst open. "Chief, come quick," Flick said. "Dispatch is reporting a 911 phone call from your house." The county didn't have a 911 dispatch center, so all emergency calls in the area went straight to Serenity Springs's police station. "It's your daughter. She wants to talk to you."

Telling himself not to panic, Jack stalked down the hall and grabbed the headset from the officer manning the dispatch desk. "Emma? Are you there? It's Daddy. Tell me what's going on."

At the silence on the other end of the line he had to swallow back his fear. "Emma? Can you hear—"

"Kelsey's hurt," Emma whimpered.

His hand trembled and he closed it into a tight fist. "What do you mean she's hurt? Is she there? Can I talk to her?"

"I heard a noise and I went downstairs to get you but you weren't there."

"I know, honey," he soothed. "I had to come in to work but Kelsey's there with you. Now, tell me how is Kelsey hurt? Did she fall?"

"N-no. The bad lady hurt her."

Jack's blood turned to ice. "Did the bad lady see you?" he asked, his heart in his throat.

"I don't think so."

He shut his eyes. "Good. Where are you right now?"

"In your closet."

"Is the door shut?"

"Yes," she said in a little voice.

"Stay there," he ordered. "Don't leave that spot. Curl up real tight in a ball in the corner and push the clothes in front of you like you did that time we played hide-and-seek. Remember, when I couldn't find you and you fell asleep?"

She sniffled. "Uh-huh."

"I'll be there to get you in a few minutes. I'm going to give the phone back to Officer Coffman, he'll talk to you until I get there."

"I want to talk to you," Emma cried.

His heart broke cleanly in two. "I know, but you have to be brave," he told her, struggling to keep his voice even and reassuring. "I'm coming to get you, but you have to stay hidden. If you hear anyone come upstairs, stay as quiet and still as possible, okay? Don't hang up the phone and don't open the door to anyone but me."

"Not even Kelsey?"

"No. Only me. Understand?"

"Yes, Daddy."

"I love you, baby," he said hoarsely. "I'll be there soon."

Handing the headset over to Coffman was one of the hardest things he'd ever done. He flexed and straightened his fingers, wanting nothing more than to take his tangled feelings out on the nearest wall.

Instead, he released a shaky breath. He wouldn't lose control. Not now.

Kelsey and Emma needed him.

He just prayed like hell he wasn't too late.

CHAPTER SEVENTEEN

KELSEY STRUGGLED AGAINST the need to slide into unconsciousness again. Something urgent, almost panic-like niggled at the edge of her brain. But it hurt to think, to remember why she couldn't simply slip back into the dark.

All she knew was that she had to get up. Emma needed her.

Pain radiating through her body, she slit her eyes open and groaned as her head spun sickeningly. Gasoline fumes assaulted her. She squeezed her eyes shut. Swallowing the urge to throw up, she concentrated on breathing through her mouth until the feeling passed.

"Get up," somebody snarled, and Kelsey opened her eyes. Turning her head slightly, her vision wavered and then focused on the pointed toes of a pair of red cowboy boots.

And that's when she remembered. The mayor had hit her with something. More than likely the butt of the gun now pointed at Kelsey's head.

Her thoughts bounced around in her aching head like bumper cars. She grimaced at the smell of acrid fumes. What the hell was going on? And where was Emma? Was she safe?

"I said, get up." This time, the mayor compounded her command with a hard kick to Kelsey's ribs.

Pain exploded in her side, knocked her breath away. She rolled over slowly and managed to get to her hands and knees. That's when her gaze caught on something red in the living-room doorway. A gas can lying on its side. And a puddle underneath the can's open spout was trailing liquid across the hardwood floor to the sofa.

A chill raced through her. The mayor was going to burn Jack's house down.

Kelsey couldn't let that happen. And what about Emma? No way would she let anything happen to that little girl. Taking shallow breaths—each one causing a sharp, stabbing pain in her chest—she struggled to her feet.

"What the hell are you doing?" Kelsey rasped. She swayed, regained her balance and lifted her hand to her head, wincing as she touched the large, tender bump. When she brought her hand down, her fingers were sticky with blood.

"Protecting what's mine," the mayor said. She waved the gun toward the kitchen. "Let's go."

When Kelsey remained frozen, the mayor raised both of her painted-on eyebrows. Using her free hand, she dug into the front pocket of her jeans and produced a Zippo lighter.

"Unless you want me to burn this dump to the ground, Jack's pretty little daughter with it, you'll do what I say."

Fear, unlike any she'd ever known, gripped her. The look in the mayor's eyes convinced her the woman wouldn't hesitate to hurt Emma.

"Why are you doing this?" Kelsey asked. She glanced around furtively but couldn't see a way to make a run for it. No way for her to get to Emma.

She needed to calm down. Allie would be there in a matter of minutes. All Kelsey had to do was stall the mayor and keep her occupied and away from that gasoline—away from Emma—until help arrived.

She only prayed Emma didn't wake up and come downstairs. *Please, God, let her sleep through this. Keep her safe.*

"Why?" the mayor repeated, her expression cold. "If it weren't for you, Jack would've done his job a week ago and your worthless brother would be behind bars. Now," she said, aiming the gun at Kelsey's head, "move."

"Look, I know you want the murderer found, but you don't have to do this." Kelsey placed a hand against the wall to keep from falling over as she edged down the hallway. "I'll leave town. I'll leave Jack. He'll arrest the right person."

"It's too late. Jack wants to try and pin this murder on *my* son, and I'm not about to let that happen."

"Jack arrested your son for the murder?"

"The only person going to be arrested for that slut's murder will be your brother." The mayor's eyes flashed. "I'm going to make sure of it."

Kelsey stumbled, catching herself on the doorjamb before she fell. "I know this must be hard for you, accepting that your son might be guilty, but I don't think this is going to help him."

"Don't be stupid," the mayor snapped. "Ben didn't kill anyone, he couldn't. Least of all that slut. Even if she did use him, and hurt him. I warned him to stay away from her. Warned her, too. But she didn't know what was good for her."

Obviously there had been no love lost between the two women. Jeez, the mayor sounded like a jealous wife or something.

Or an overprotective mama.

"Oh my God," Kelsey breathed as the realization dawned. "*You* killed her."

"I told her to stay away from Ben, but she wanted to take him away from me. I did what I had to do to protect him."

"How is hurting me going to help your son?" Kelsey backed into the kitchen. "If you want to help him, you should turn yourself in. Admit what you've done—"

"Why should I turn myself in when by tomorrow morning your brother will be arrested for Shannon's murder?" the mayor said as she advanced, the gun in her hand rock steady. She grinned. "And yours?"

"No one will believe Dillon hurt me."

"Once they find the gas can with his fingerprints all over it, they will. And when they discover your body in that disgusting bar, killed by your brother's own hammer, well, even Jack Martin won't be able to dispute the evidence."

Fear coated Kelsey's mouth. "Jack will see through this, and when he does, he'll come after you with everything he's got."

"You're making yourself more important than you are," the mayor said, creeping closer until Kelsey was backed against the counter. "I know all about you. You have nothing, no family, no parents or friends. You're nobody."

No! Kelsey's heart screamed even as her stomach sank. That's not true. She wasn't alone. She had hope she and Dillon could work out their problems. And she had Jack and Emma.

And she'd be damned if she'd let this murderer take that away from her.

With an effort, Kelsey lifted her chin. "Jack will care."

The mayor shook her head. When she spoke, her voice was almost pitying. "You'd like to think that, wouldn't you? You don't belong here. You're not a part of this town or Jack's family. No one cares if you live or die."

A movement on the front porch caught Kelsey's attention. "Wanna bet?"

Two seconds later, the door was kicked open. The mayor spun around, aiming her gun at Jack. Kelsey launched herself at the other woman, wrapped her arms around the mayor's waist and sent them both crashing to the ground.

The mayor shrieked and scrambled to get up, her elbow connecting with the side of Kelsey's head. Kelsey's vision swam. By the time she'd focused again, it was to see the mayor pressed face-first against the wall, her hands behind her as Jack cuffed her.

Kelsey licked her dry lips and struggled to remain awake. "Emma," she said, but her voice was little more than a whisper and she wasn't sure Jack even heard her. The last thing she remembered was the sight of Jack rushing to her side, and then everything went dark.

"WHAT THE HELL WERE YOU thinking?" Jack demanded twenty minutes later as he paced in front of the porch step where Kelsey had just been attended to by an EMT.

They'd opened all the windows and doors and had hauled out the gasoline-soaked furniture, but the house still reeked with fumes, forcing them outside.

Emma tightened her hold on his neck and he automatically patted her back. She'd clung to him like a burr ever since he'd found her tucked away in the corner of his closet. Not that he minded. Hell, it might be a day or two before he was ready to let go of his little girl again.

Mindful of the fact that they weren't alone, he lowered his voice as he said, "You could've been killed."

She looked up at him, a blanket draped over her shoulders.

The bandage the EMT had applied to her head wound was stark-white against the brightness of her hair. Even though she was safe and whole and alive, the sight of an ugly, purple bruise on her face renewed Jack's rage. He knew she had a larger, worse bruise on her side, thanks to the pointy toes of Christine's boots.

He'd come so close to losing both Emma and Kelsey.

"I wasn't thinking," Kelsey admitted. "I just sort of… reacted. I was afraid she would shoot at you. And, well, to be honest, she was really pissing me off."

He shook his head. He shifted Emma to his hip, crouched in front of Kelsey and reached for her hand. "You scared the hell out of me," he admitted quietly.

"Sorry." She glanced at Emma. Reached out her free hand as if to touch his daughter, only to lower it to her lap. "Are you sure she's okay?"

He squeezed Kelsey's fingers. "She seems to be. Knowing you're all right went a long way toward calming her down."

Emma raised her head again and told Kelsey, "The bad lady's going to Daddy's jail."

"That's right," Jack said, "and she won't be coming back here. Ever."

Kelsey smiled and smoothed Emma's sleep-tousled hair. "You're a hero."

"I am?" Emma asked, her eyes wide as she looked from Jack to Kelsey. "Just like Daddy?"

Kelsey nodded. "It was very smart of you to remember to call 911. And very brave."

"I was real scared." Emma's grip on Jack tightened, her lower lip began to quiver.

Kelsey laid her hand on Emma's shoulder. "But you still

called for help. That's what being brave is. Doing something even though you're scared."

Emma slid a sideways glance at Jack. "Like getting your ears pierced even though you know it's gonna hurt but not crying 'cuz it's something you really, *really* want and you'll be real 'sponsible and clean your ears every day?"

Kelsey burst into laugher.

"What?" Emma wanted to know.

Jack couldn't contain his own grin. "How about we discuss the whole ear-piercing issue tomorrow?"

Emma's eyes lit up. "Really, Daddy?"

"I said discuss it," Jack reminded her. "I didn't say yes."

"I know, Daddy." But Emma grinned and laid her head back on his shoulder as if she knew damn well he was going to give in.

He and Kelsey looked at each other.

"I thought I'd lost both of you," he said hoarsely.

Kelsey's eyes watered. "I was so scared Emma was going to get hurt," she whispered. "I swear to you, Jack, I would've done anything to keep her safe."

"I know." He raised their joined hands and kissed her knuckles. "Thank you."

She pulled her hand back to wipe away her tears. "I still can't believe the mayor killed Shannon and almost killed me."

Jack grunted. He couldn't believe it, either. And damn if he didn't blame himself for not seeing the connection between Christine, Ben and Shannon earlier.

"It's not your fault," Kelsey said.

"Are you a mind reader, now?"

"I don't know about reading minds but I can easily read

your face." She traced her fingertips over his cheek. "You realized it was the mayor."

"Yeah, but I was almost too late."

"You weren't," she said simply.

Jack nodded, knowing the fact that both Kelsey and Emma were alive and safe was going to have to be enough. For now.

He stood, pulled out his cell phone and pushed a button.

"Who are you calling?" Kelsey asked.

"Allie. As much as I hate to leave Emma—or you—I need to get down to the station. And, no," he said when Kelsey opened her mouth, "you are not staying here with her. The house is going to need to be professionally cleaned to get rid of the gasoline and you're going to the hospital."

"But, Jack I—"

"No arguing." Allie's answering machine picked up and he frowned.

"Jack!" Allie shouted as she hurried up his walkway.

Clicking off his phone, he returned the hug she gave him.

"Sweetie, are you okay?" she asked as Emma went into her aunt's outstretched arms. Allie looked to Jack. "Is everyone all right?"

"Everyone's fine." He took hold of Allie's elbow and led her into the yard. "But how did you find out so quickly? Please don't tell me it's already spreading around town."

"What? No. I didn't know anything about it until I got here." Allie smoothed her hand over Emma's back. "I spoke with Pascale, he's monitoring traffic at the end of the street. He filled me in."

"Then what are you doing here?"

"Kelsey called and said you needed me to sit with Emma."

"When?"

Allie frowned at his abrupt tone. "About forty minutes ago, maybe longer. I would've been here sooner but I was just getting out of the shower when she called and—"

"Kelsey asked you to stay here? With Emma?"

"Yes and yes." She looked at him as if he was speaking in tongues. "Are you sure you're all right?"

"Fine," he managed. But he wasn't fine. Not by a long shot. So much for things working out between him and Kelsey.

He glanced back to the porch to see the EMTs helping Kelsey to her feet. She obviously didn't want anything to do with the stretcher they'd brought in. She looked over at him, surprise and something else, something like guilt, in her expression.

"Wait," she said to the EMT holding her arm. "Jack, I can explain—"

"No need," he told her, keeping his face expressionless. "I'll have one of my officers contact you for a full statement about what happened here tonight."

She reached out for him. "Jack, please—"

She broke off when he stepped back. She didn't want him. Not enough to stay.

He'd told her if she wanted to leave, he wouldn't stand in her way. So he let her go. "Goodbye, Kelsey."

JACK KNEW SHE'D BEEN READY to run. Kelsey rolled her eyes and instantly regretted it, overwhelmed by dizziness. Of course he knew, she thought as she regained her equilibrium. He'd spoken to Allie, hadn't he? He'd found out firsthand she'd called his sister to stay with Emma so she could take off. But what he didn't know was that she'd changed her mind. She had to find him, to explain that she'd made a mistake.

She wasn't going anywhere.

Well, except out of this hospital room.

If only she could get her damn jeans on. It had taken a good fifteen minutes, but she'd managed to unhook her IV, get out of bed and get her right leg into her pants. The E.R. doctor had cut her shirt off to avoid jarring her side any more than necessary, but she figured she'd just put her jacket over the hospital gown. Once she had both legs in her pants, that is.

Supporting her weight on the bed, she attempted to lift her left foot, only to lower it with a gasp.

"Going somewhere?"

She caught her breath at the sound of Jack's voice. Turning slowly, carefully, she spotted him in the doorway. His hair was disheveled, his shirt wrinkled and lines of fatigue bracketed his mouth.

But none of that mattered. He was there and, whether he knew it or not, all hers.

"Actually," she said, "I was going—"

"To take off without being discharged?" He crossed the room and scowled down at her. He looked so exhausted. "Don't be an idiot."

"Who are you calling an idiot?"

"You. And it fits if you think you should be going anywhere with a concussion and a cracked rib. Get back into bed."

"Are you here for anything specific? Or just to let me know how stupid you think I am?"

He crossed his arms and frowned. "I ran into Dillon out in the hallway."

Her mouth popped open. "What? Dillon was here? Why?"

"He heard what happened and was worried about you."

"Yeah, right," she scoffed and sharp pain shot through her chest.

"He asked about you. And he wanted me to tell you he's glad you're okay."

Dillon hadn't even taken the time to see her himself, but he had come to ask about her. Maybe he had been worried. It was such a little thing, but it gave her hope.

She bent down to pull her pants up and heard Jack curse under his breath. Gritting her teeth she lifted her foot only to have Jack kneel down and gently guide her foot into the leg opening of her jeans. She straightened slowly, her eyes on the top of his head as he pulled the denim up her legs and over her hips.

His large, warm hands settled at her waist. She raised her head to find Jack's face mere inches from her own. Maybe she didn't need to tell him how she felt. Maybe she could show him.

But just as she stretched up, he stepped back, his hands falling from her waist.

"The D.A. is charging Christine with first-degree murder."

She kept her eyes down and fought back tears as she tugged at her zipper. "That was fast."

"He thinks he can prove that Christine became enraged after seeing her son's car at Shannon's—especially since she'd warned Shannon to stay away from him. Christine's lawyer is already making noises about a plea bargain—"

"So she could get away with it?" Kelsey asked in disbelief.

"Doubtful," Jack said, his voice even. "We have enough

evidence that the D.A. thinks he can prove Christine went to Shannon's with the intent to kill. And that she did everything in her power to set your brother up to take the fall."

Her eyes widened. "What?"

"The story Dora ran in the paper last Sunday? Seems Christine was Dora's anonymous source. She got her information from Ben and then did her best to convince the community of Ward's guilt. She must've hoped it would pressure me into making an arrest."

"That bitch," she murmured vehemently, clenching her fingers. "You just can't trust a politician, can you?"

"No, ma'am. I guess sometimes you can't."

Ma'am? Kelsey's gaze shot to his face. Oh, this was bad. He was wearing his cop mask—calm, cool and, worst of all, emotionless.

"Is that…" She stopped. "Is…that the only reason you're here? To tell me about the mayor?"

He studied her intently. "What other reason could there be?" he asked quietly.

She bit her lower lip. "Look, I freaked, okay?"

"I'm not sure I know what you mean."

"Yes, you do."

"Why don't you clarify it for me?"

Damn him. He was being stubborn. And a bit mean. Worse, she knew she deserved both. "I called Allie because… because even if what we shared was incredible, and it was, or is, or whatever—"

"Slow down," he soothed. "Shallow breaths."

She nodded but that made her head hurt again. "Being with you makes me feel…content and…and whole. Like when I'm not with you, a piece of me is missing."

"And that bothers you?"

"I don't want someone to hold that much power over me. I don't want to give that much of myself away." She wished she could pace, but even the effort of standing was beginning to take its toll. "I'm…I'm not cut out for it. I'm sure as hell not any good at it and…I'm scared."

Hurt flashed over his face. "Of me?"

"No. God no. I'm scared of screwing this up. Of hurting you and Emma. I don't know the first thing about loving someone. I don't…I don't think I know how." Tears rolled down her cheeks. "But when I imagine my life without you and Emma, I don't like what I see."

"So, instead of trying, you were going to leave?"

"I panicked. I mean…we've known each other barely two weeks." She forced herself to tell him everything. "But I love you, Jack. I've never said that to anyone before," she added quickly. "Besides Dillon, I don't think I've ever felt it for anyone before. I don't…I don't know if that'll be enough for this to work. But I'm willing to give it a try. I want us to try."

He stepped closer, his expression serious. "Okay."

"I—" She blinked and rubbed at the wetness on her cheeks. "Huh? Okay?"

He sifted his fingers through her hair. "I love you, too."

He moved to kiss her but she pressed a hand to his chest. "Wait a minute. That's it? Just okay, I love you, too? I thought you were mad."

"I was."

She pressed her lips together. "You gave me the go-ahead to leave, remember?"

"I changed my mind."

"Just like that?"

"Pretty much. I don't want to spend the rest of my life wondering if I made a mistake by letting you go without a fight." He shrugged, looking decidedly less tired than he had a few minutes ago. "So I came over here to fight for you."

"You did?"

He grinned. "I had it all worked out. I was going to tell you how we mean something to each other. How I know you feel it, too. That I find you sexy, funny and intelligent. You survived abuse, neglect and disappointment and it's only made you stronger, more determined to become a better person."

"And you thought that would work?"

"If not, I was just going to tell you that I love you. Lucky for me, you came to your senses first."

"Yeah," she groused. "Lucky you."

He chuckled and leaned forward to press a soft kiss against her mouth. "I would've fought for you, Kelsey," he whispered. He pulled back and searched her face. "You belong here with me. Will you stay? Will you be a part of my life, of Emma's life?"

"I'll stay," she told him, thrilled and humbled by the love she saw in his eyes. Love for her. She smiled letting him see how happy he made her. "Besides, I've been wanting to check out those handcuffs of yours."

"You up for a game of cop and troublemaker?"

"You bet." Kelsey was filled with joy and love. And for the first time in her life, contentment. "But I get to be the sheriff."

* * * * *

Love Inspired
HISTORICAL

*Powerful, engaging stories of romance, adventure and faith
set in the past—when life was simpler and faith played a
major role in everyday lives.*

*See below for a sneak preview of
HIGH COUNTRY BRIDE
by Jillian Hart*

*Love Inspired Historical—love and faith
throughout the ages*

Silence remained between them, and she felt the rake of his gaze, taking her in from the top of her wind-blown hair where escaped tendrils snapped in the wind to the toe of her scuffed, patched shoes. She watched him fist up his big, work-roughened hands and expected the worst.

"You never told me, Miz Nelson. Where are you going to go?" His tone was flat, his jaw tensed as if he were still fighting his temper. His blue gaze shot past her to watch the children going about their picking up.

"I don't know." Her throat went dry. Her tongue felt thick as she answered. "When I find employment, I could wire a payment to you. Rent. Y-you aren't think-ing of bringing the sher-rif in?"

"You think I want *payment?*" He boomed like winter thunder. *"You think I want rent money?"*

"Frankly, I don't know what you want."

"I'll tell you what I don't want. I don't want—" His words cannoned in the silence as he paused, and a passing pair of geese overhead honked in flat-noted tones. He grimaced, and it was impossible to know what he would say or do.

She trembled, not from fear of him, she truly didn't believe he would strike her, but from the unknown. Of being forced to take the frightening step off the only safe spot she'd known since she'd lost Pa's house.

When you were homeless, everything seemed so fragile, so easily off balance, for it was a big, unkind world for a woman alone with her children. She had no one to protect her. No one to care. The truth was, she'd never had those things in her husband. How could she expect them from any stranger? Especially this man she hardly knew, who was harsh and cold and hard-hearted.

And, worse, what if he brought in the law?

"You can't keep living out of a wagon," he said, still angry, the cords still straining in his neck. "Animals have enough sense to keep their young cared for and safe."

Yes, it was as she'd thought. He intended to be as cruel about this as he could be. She spun on her heel, pulling up all her defenses, and was determined to let his upcoming hurtful words roll off her like rainwater on an oiled tarp. She grabbed the towel the children had neatly folded and tossed it into the laundry box in the back of the wagon.

"Miz Nelson. I'm talking to you."

"Yes, I know. If you expect me to stand there while you tongue lash me, you're mistaken. I have packing to get to." Her fingers were clumsy as she hefted the bucket of water she'd brought for washing—she wouldn't need that now—and heaved.

His hand clasped on the handle beside hers, and she could feel the life and power of him vibrate along the thin metal. "Give it to me."

Her fingers let go. She felt stunned as he walked away, easily carrying the bucket that had been so heavy to her, and quietly, methodically, put out the small cooking fire. He did not seem as ominous or as intimidating—somehow—as he stood in the shadows, bent to his task, although she couldn't say why that was. Perhaps it was because he wasn't acting the way she was used to men acting. She was quite used to doing all the work.

Jamie scurried over, juggling his wooden horses, to watch. Daisy hung back, eyes wide and still, taking in the mysterious goings-on.

He is different when he's near to them, she realized. He didn't seem harsh, and there was no hint of anger—or, come to think of it, any other emotion—as he shook out the empty bucket, nodded once to the children and then retraced his path to her.

"Let me guess." He dropped the bucket onto the tailgate, and his anger appeared to be back. Cords strained in his neck and jaw as he growled at her. "If you leave here, you don't know where you're going and you have no money to get there with?"

She nodded. "Yes, sir."

"Then get you and your kids into the wagon. I'll hitch up your horses for you." His eyes were cold and yet they were not unfeeling as he fastened his gaze on hers. "I have an empty shanty out back of my house that no one's living in. You can stay there for the night."

"What?" She stumbled back, and the solid wood of the tailgate bit into the small of her back. "But—"

"There will be no argument," he bit out, interrupting her. "None at all. I buried a wife and son years ago, what was most

precious to me, and to see you and them neglected like this—
with no one to care—" His jaw ground again and his eyes
were no longer cold.

Joanna didn't think she'd ever seen anything sadder than
Aiden McKaslin as the sun went down on him.

* * * * *

Don't miss this deeply moving story,
HIGH COUNTRY BRIDE,
available July 2008
from the new Love Inspired Historical line.

Also look for
SEASIDE CINDERELLA
by Anna Schmidt,
where a poor servant girl and a wealthy merchant prince
might somehow make a life together.

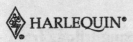

SAVE $1.00

A riveting trilogy from
BRENDA NOVAK

SAVE $1.00 on the purchase price of one book in **The Last Stand** trilogy from Brenda Novak.

Offer valid from May 27, 2008, to August 30, 2008.
Redeemable at participating retail outlets. Limit one coupon per purchase.

52608328

5 65373 00076 2 (8100) 0 11499

® and TM are trademarks owned and used by the trademark owner and/or its licensee.
© 2008 Harlequin Enterprises Limited

MBNTRI08CPN

Lawyer Audrey Lincoln has sworn off love, throwing herself into her work instead. When she meets a much younger cop named Ryan Mercedes, all her logic is tossed out the window, and Ryan is determined that he will not let the issue of age come between them. It is not until a tragic case involving an innocent child threatens to tear them apart that Ryan and Audrey must fight for a way to finally be together....

Look for

TRUSTING RYAN

by Tara Taylor Quinn

Available July
wherever you buy books.

HARLEQUIN Super Romance

COMING NEXT MONTH

#1500 TRUSTING RYAN • Tara Taylor Quinn
For Detective Ryan Mercedes, right and wrong are clear. And what he feels for guardian ad litem Audrey Lincoln is very right. Their shared pursuit of justice proves they're on the same side. But when a case divides them, can he see things her way?

#1501 A MARRIAGE BETWEEN FRIENDS • Melinda Curtis
Marriage of Inconvenience
They were friends who married when Jill needed a father for her unborn child, and Vince offered his name. Then, unexpectedly, Jill walked out. Now, eleven years later, Vince Patrizio is back to reclaim his wife...and the son who should have been theirs.

#1502 HIS SON'S TEACHER • Kay Stockham
The Tulanes of Tennessee
Nick Tulane has never fallen for a teacher. A former dropout, he doesn't go for the academic type. Until he meets Jennifer Rose, that is. While she's busy helping his son catch up at school, Nick starts wishing for some private study time with the tutor.

#1503 THE CHILD COMES FIRST • Elizabeth Ashtree
Star defense attorney Simon Montgomery is called upon to defend a girl who claims to be wrongly accused of murder. Her social worker Jayda Kavanagh believes she's innocent. But as Simon and Jayda grow close trying to save the child, Jayda's own youthful trauma could stand between her and the love Simon offers.

#1504 NOBODY'S HERO • Carrie Alexander
Count on a Cop
Massachusetts state police officer Sean Rafferty has sworn off ever playing hero again. All he wants is to be left alone to recover. Which is perfect, because Connie Bradford doesn't need a hero in her life. Unfortunately, her grieving daughter does...

#1505 THE WAY HOME • Jean Brashear
Everlasting Love
They'd been everything to each other. But Bella Parker—stricken with amnesia far from home—can't remember any of it...not even the betrayal that made her leave. Now James Parker has to decide how much of their past he should tell her. Because the one piece that could jog her memory might destroy them forever.

HSRCNM0608